MY FAVORITE GIRLFRIEND WAS A FRENCH BULLDOG

McSWEENEY'S
SAN FRANCISCO

Cover illustration by Laurent Moreau

McSweeney's and colophon are registered trademarks of McSweeney's, a privately held company with wildly fluctuating resources.

Printed in Canada

ISBN: 978-1-944211-77-6

10 9 8 7 6 5 4 3 2 1

www.mcsweeneys.net

MY FAVORITE GIRLFRIEND WAS A FRENCH BULLDOG

LEGNA RODRÍGUEZ IGLESIAS

Translation by Megan McDowell

McSWEENEY'S
SAN FRANCISCO

Any resemblance to actual events can be blamed on me. I don't care.

*My favorite girlfriend was
a French bulldog.
When I scolded her,
she peed herself.*

POLITICS

I died six months after turning ninety years old. Of meningoencephalitis. In a Military Hospital close to the old quarter, one kilometer from the Zoo and the Casino Campestre park. I left behind a wife, three children, five grandchildren, and two great-grandchildren. Later on, more great-grandchildren will be born, my wife will die, my children will grow old. Everything at its own pace. In natural and chronological order.

Everyone thought it was a cold, with all the fevers and shaking, but it was meningo. They saw my wracking shivers and they were scared, but that's the way colds always are. The body shuts down, the head aches, the temperature rises, the jaw and hands start to shake.

Since I'm dead I don't feel a thing; free of sensation, I enjoy the show. My wife, an elderly woman not five feet tall, is sitting at the table when my daughter comes to give her the news that I've passed on. My favorite granddaughters, the ones my wife and I raised, are laughing in the spare room. It's nervous laughter. Laughter that means *I can't believe it*. The dogs know I'm here, sitting in the same place as always.

When I die they cover me with a sheet. They take me to the morgue, cut me open. They take a saw to my head. They close me up in the same places they opened me. They shake me. My daughter arrives to fix me up. She cries while she dresses me. She combs my hair like I'm a child. She buttons my shirt. Zips up my pants. Adjusts my belt. She lays her head on my chest. I'm her father.

My daughter realizes they left my pacemaker in. She wants to call them back, but it's only an impulse, none of them are about to open me up to remove the little metal object. The pacemaker will go on working until it rusts out underground. The other dead people, the ones around me, won't be able to sleep in peace. I won't be able to sleep either. I'm not sleepy. Or afraid.

The other dead people, compared to me, don't deserve mourning or a wake; that's what my family and friends think when they arrive and snoop around the rest of the funeral home. They peer in and show off, they're shameless.

Two years later, when the cemetery supervisors and my family members—which will be only my daughter, as always—dig up my remains and put my ashes in a small box they can pay their respects to whenever they visit the cemetery, the pacemaker will be intact. It'll even shine, like a thought, clear and lucid.

My daughter arrives home with her mouth contorted. Her eyes red and watery. Everyone realizes I have died. Except my wife, a naive woman. For a while now she's needed everything to be explained at length. So they explain to her that I am a very strong man, but meningoencephalitis is stronger than me. She understands. She promises not to make a scene. Not to cry. She remembers me, her husband. Her companion for over seventy years.

I was born on January twenty-fifth, nineteen nineteen, in a rural area far from sea and city. I worked in the fields, under the rain, from the time I turned six years old. At that age I started to smoke—black tobacco—so I wouldn't faint on the road.

In nineteen thirty-six, when the war broke out, I started to fight for the Republic alongside of a group of compañeros of an origin different from those who didn't fight. My origin. Taking part in protests and collecting relief funds. My parents, of the same humble origin, just kept quiet.

I learned that a man is a country. I learned that a country is a system. I learned that a system is a monster. I learned that a monster is a God. I learned that God doesn't exist. I learned that God does exist. I learned that I don't exist. I learned that I do exist. I learned that a man cannot leave, because this is his house, this is his mother, and this is his father.

In nineteen forty-six and in nineteen forty-seven I was pursued and imprisoned by the forces of the Regime of the Moment as a result of my active participation in defensive, rebellious actions. I got to know the smells of prison, absolute darkness, the sun. I urinated and defecated on myself. Prisons like El Príncipe, El Presidio Modelo, and Francisquito all saw me enter and leave, through a narrow door, transformed into a man.

When I got out of prison I went on with the same things. The scars under my skin then were vital, attractive. The

Military Socialist Party and all things like it became my home, my domain. During that time and after nineteen fifty-two, I organized secret, clandestine meetings under my own roof, and I had to take measures to keep us from being discovered. None of this would have been possible without my wife, my love. She went out to get food and prepared it, she distributed the plates, kissed and hugged me from a place high up, unknown. Her kiss was bread and water.

When the attack on the country's most important barracks occurred, the Party directed me to enter a Religious Order, to get access to the printing press where they made flyers and other kinds of propaganda that I then distributed. I didn't believe in God, and the members of the Order saw in my eyes the eyes of a more or less ferocious beast.

That's what I am and that's what my sons and my daughter are, and that's what my sons' sons and my daughter's daughters are: more or less ferocious beasts.

We made charcoal in our house, my wife and I, together. We lived off the trees and off of love. In the name of those trees I brought fire to other houses, food. I collected money, clothes, and arms. Under the charcoal, on my cart, I transported and delivered the wares. My wife went with me many times on my rounds in the city and to other nearby places. And she herself left weapons, there, where no one would know.

As Council President, with support from my wife and those who elected me, I built a School that is still our community's school today. The schoolyard doesn't have flowers—it must be the heat, or the earth, but it used to have them.

In nineteen seventy, after the Triumph, I directed the province's charcoal co-ops, taking part in the supervision and organization of the other workers. I saw the foundations, the light, the universe.

I never accepted offers to live in confiscated houses. I built my own home with wooden beams and planks. Two rooms and a door were enough. My children wanted more but I didn't give them more. My children's children wanted more but I didn't give them more. My daughter's daughters, when they were born, would have liked more. I gave them what was necessary. My wife kept quiet, lowered her eyes, gave me her hand. The bones of her hand between the bones of mine.

I went on founding, directing, lending a hand. Every man is the continuation of another man, just as every action is the continuation of another action. That's what I did and would still be doing, if the meningo hadn't dragged me off feet first, if it hadn't brought me here.

Meningoencephalitis is an illness that simultaneously recalls both forms of meningitis. It occurs through an infection or inflammation of the meninges, and through an infection or inflammation of the brain. There are many organisms that cause it, both viral and bacterial pathogens, and there are parasitic, treacherous microbes. The illness has high mortality rates and severe morbidity. The body shuts down, the head aches, the temperature rises, the jaw and hands start to shake.

For me, who suffered and endured this illness, it has a lot in common with revolution. The human body is the system against which the revolution fights, clandestinely at first and then in a more organized, visible, and public manner, in the end laying waste to it. The body shuts down, the head aches, the temperature rises, the jaw and hands start to shake.

The cemetery is the final place that the body, revolutionary and cold, will occupy. There are dry flowers everywhere, and the body senses that. The sensations continue a little while after the corporal break that a demise entails. The revolution that has reached its apogee in the body stays alive for some days, and that's why the body disintegrates—because a very rebellious thing is writhing inside as it tries to move on to another phase.

This other phase is nullity. Trying to vanquish the revolution is categorically forbidden; however, as soon as the body realizes it exists, that's exactly what it does. Its stamp, its reality, has no precedent in the body. From there comes the definitive event that establishes a base in the body for colonization and radicalization. The family does not exist. It's just you, either for it or against it. You join or you resist, Resistance that in the long run grants it a measure of strength.

The funeral home—an old, enormous house, previously the property of some bourgeois family—has been recently painted. It boasts a bathroom and a cafe, but both have deteriorated to the point where they can no longer perform their functions. I—a body that is also old—am resting in one of the chapels. Other cadavers round out the class. They are of different types, sexes, and ages. My cadaver is without a doubt the least young of them all.

There are few people during the night. When morning

comes they start arriving, in groups or in families. They all keep vigil over their dead. They are all the same.

My chapel has the most people. Even in such a solemn moment as this one, people feel pride. My family is proud. You can see it in their eyes, in the way they hold vigil over me and sit down to wait by my side, next to the coffin. Children, grandchildren, nieces and nephews, cousins. They all have a vain air, a self-important attitude, bless them.

Someone is missing and it's my wife. The only person I wouldn't have wanted to miss it, at my side always. She can't get up from her rocker. Nor will she be able to. After a few days or weeks have passed, most likely she'll fracture a hip going out to get lunch. These things happen, especially during mourning, in sadness.

I know there are flowers, shields and flags. There are medals on my casket. Six of them. Honors that I deserved, that I kept safe. Now my daughter will keep them and then my granddaughter, the one who doesn't believe in what I believe in. The one who laughs at me. The one who cries the most. The one who won't be dragged away from the coffin. There are three, really.

The national flag hides the coffin's nails from view. My daughter spread it over the casket, lengthwise and side to side.

I've never seen a flag like that. I bristle. The nails are tiny little points that you can see anyway. The casket, made of bad wood, is lined with black cloth. The cloth is tacked with lace, but it has no elegance. That's what bothers the cadaver's family.

My daughter didn't want too many flowers because there was only one kind: ugly, purple and blue flowers. Ones that fill the space with an almost unbearable cemetery smell. It smells of cemetery anyway. My sons go far away in search of flowers. They want flowers at any cost. But the flowers don't matter at all. Only the flag is important. And the medals. And the family. They find lilies. My daughter contents herself with lilies.

One of the little girls never stops looking at me. She peers through the coffin's glass and thinks she sees two ants in my hair. The ants run about as if my hair were grass. My daughter calls to her and she doesn't go. Of all those present, she will be the only one to tell the story. She was born for that. To tell the story. It's possible, even, that she'll spend her whole life telling stories that aren't hers.

I try to think
that writing
this book
in some vintage glasses
is the best thing
that's ever happened to me.
The more I think,
the more tears I shed.

MONSTER

In any case, my case would be first on a list of exceptional cases you couldn't make much of a case for, since it is an exception—though not the only one, for worse or for better—and is in the minority.

At an exact time and place, my application—endorsed by an institution—would have to be duly received by a security guard who would make sure to look me in the eye and check that my expression coincided with its counterpart on an identity document, which two seconds earlier I would have deposited in his hands. Likewise, others in front of me and behind me would behave in exactly the same way.

I moved forward a block until I reached the next security guard, who, like the previous one, asked for my ID and those of the others, again focusing in on my appearance and the appearances of the rest. I slid my hand into my bag and turned off my phone without the guard noticing any movement. "Does anyone have a phone?" he asked, and, shyly, I raised the same hand that seconds before I'd slid into my bag. The guard smiled. "Go across the street," he told me, "and leave it in *that house*." I didn't understand. I quickly calculated how much my phone had cost me: between the price of the phone itself and the fee for a number, it was a hundred and sixty total, the same amount I would hand over before being questioned in just a few short moments. "You can't go in with a phone," the guard ordered, "not on or off, no phones." I crossed the street and stopped in front of the house. A woman emerged from inside and reached out her hand so I could give her the phone, my phone, trustingly. In exchange for my phone she gave me a token. "Number twenty, don't lose it," the woman added. *Don't lose the phone*, I thought as I put the token in my pocket. A dirty token, made of wood, pine, the number twenty almost imperceptible. I turned around in a hurry, not wanting to get separated from my institutional group. "Don't cross," cried the guard. "You have to go back to the corner, report to the guard booth, then advance slowly back to this point. No running allowed."

A park two blocks from the Office serves as a waiting room for the general population. Cameras atop electrical poles abound in the park, and officials dressed in civilian clothes spread out among the population and inform the Office if any plot or rumor starts to spread. Most of the people congregated in the park begin to sit down on the sidewalk once they see that time keeps passing and they still aren't called. Large rocks also serve as seats. The elderly grow desperate and some of them suffer fits, their blood pressure rises or drops, they cry. Young people who grow hungry are given the option of buying sandwiches in one of the nearby cafes: cheese, ham, or ham and cheese.

No wind blows in the park, and yet, as you approach, an ocean breeze starts to rise: in the distance sea assails the shore, the sky turns gray, the breeze becomes a gust. You want to give your hand to someone, lean on someone, an individual, a citizen, preferably one sponsored by an institution.

* * *

We entered. A woman inspected my bag and found objects the Office found inappropriate for an interview. (Pencils, aloe vera hand gel, moisturizing gel for scars, Oral-B dental floss, lipstick, eyeshadow, mascara, a nail file, tweezers, Tjing Liang Yu Chinese tiger balm, flash drives, theophylline 200 mg capsules, and a thermometer. Everything a woman needs.) I received another token, and more of my belongings were detained under the reproachful eyes of my peers. *Hope they don't get lost*, I thought while I stashed the token in my pocket, feeling the two of them brush against my thigh. "Your name?" asked the woman, and I told her. "Nothing gets lost here," she added before we went up the stairs and disappeared inside through a heavy iron door that opened electronically and closed behind us like a definitive wall.

Inside, it was no worse. A lot of people in lines. Five glass windows with a hole in the center through which we would make payments. Some people, sponsored by an institution like me, paid a hundred and sixty. But not everyone paid the same, the fees went up according to the reasons for your hearing. A two-year-old girl got her leg stuck in a hole and started to cry. The leg wouldn't come out and the crying went on. The people wanted to see the girl from their seats, they craned their necks, their heads, but the girl was very small; you could only hear her sobs, the anguish. "I told you not to let go of her," a guard said to the girl's keeper while she tried to get her leg out. The guard's expression did not relieve the girl or console her keeper, rather, it upset them both more and exacerbated the accident. The leg wouldn't come out. People forgot about it. The guard made his escape. After paying, another heavy iron door and another wall. The interior of an unknown place into which we seemed to be disappearing further and further.

Wooden, yellow-painted chairs arranged to face a screen that said nothing, red, insignificant numbers. Sitting in the chairs, maybe fifty people, maybe twice as many. I was losing aptitudes.

We sat down in the same order we arrived. As a voice called our names, we got up one by one so they could take our fingerprints. First the right index, then the ring, the middle, and the pinky fingers. Then the left index, ring, middle, and pinky. Then thumbs. It took effort. It wasn't easy to press the fingertips just right. A woman was there to help us, pressing her hands down on ours. Ten fingerprints per head would make five hundred prints per half hour, more or less, not counting the institutionally sponsored prints. The scanner caught my attention, a transparent sheet that illuminated my hand when I brought it close to the light. Finally, something pleasant.

Likewise pleasant was the conversation between those who, like me, belonged to an institution. In contrast to the people who came individually to request permission, those of us with institutions had full confidence that our permits would not be refused, for obvious reasons. And our faces— those of us with institutions—displayed the calm that comes from self-confidence.

I waited my turn for approximately three hours, sitting alongside painters, filmmakers, distinguished professors, doctors, scientists, businesspeople, engineers. Our institutions favored us. It was the Ministry that protected the community of our institutions. Infinite gratitude to the Ministry, and the desire for it to continue tirelessly improving the world.

The conversations of the institutional men centered on academic subjects. A man beside me stared at my thighs, naked and pale, covered in unshaven fuzz. That was when I realized that an interview should be attended in pants or a dress, never in a garment like the pair of shorts I was wearing. The tokens in my right pocket brushed nervously against my thigh. Jangling and cold. "It's cold in here," I ventured. I crossed my legs. I bit my lip. I scratched my breast. I smiled. I asked the man what his job was, and he replied that he worked in the Ministry.

I didn't ask his name because the knowledge that he worked at the Ministry was enough. A Ministry sustains a country. Makes it strong. Establishes it. I raised my arms to the sky and gave thanks on behalf of my family and my people, and myself, to be sitting beside so important a man, someone who really honored me with his presence, his destiny.

Near us—the applicants endorsed by institutions—there were at least three windows, glassed and with their respective holes in the center, through which we could hear the voice, feminine or masculine, of the questioning person behind it. The queries, seemingly innocent, revolved around personal, almost intimate matters regarding family or work. The requested permits were for the most part denied. The citizen made a face, shed some tears, moved toward the door on the verge of collapse. "Have a good day," said the voice from the other side of the glass. "Next, please." And a similar scene played out again.

We shouldn't have had doubts about our applications: the certainty they would be granted almost won over our spirits. After all, the institutions we belonged to had already given their opinions about us. Even so, the terror showed in our eyes, our pupils wanted to dilate. The air conditioning, so pleasant at first, had taken on a wintery quality. I took off my glasses.

One by one, we of institutions went inside. Interviews short or long, frivolous or meaningful took place during a period of more or less three hours. My turn finally came, and I was called by my surname, then my first name. "Good afternoon, ma'am," I managed to hear, "how are you?" "Very well, and you?" I replied. "What is the reason for your trip, exactly?" was the first question. "It's an international event," was my reply. "And what are you?" asked the voice. I hesitated a moment at that question. I was me in all my being, I belonged to an institution that belonged to a ministry that belonged to a country, and I was proud of that, very proud. "Do you have family there?" was the third question. "No, no one." "Would you like to stay there?" "No, I wouldn't." And then, before I could even wipe my sweat away, I heard the all too familiar phrase: "Have a nice day, it's been a pleasure, next please."

If permission was granted, this phrase was preceded by another, which informed the applicant of the day and time he or she should pick up the permit. And if the applicant belonged to an institution, he or she was informed of the day and time to pick it up at the Ministry. Those words didn't come for me, and instead there was this: "Your case must be investigated at the Ministry, the Ministry will inform you."

Finally, I was given a document called Confirmation, which confirms that an application to temporarily leave the country has been submitted. Said document consists of two pages.

On the first page is a summary of passport information and, underneath, an explanatory note: *The electronic delivery of your application is the FIRST STEP in the process of applying for leave. The next step is to read the website of the place where you plan to request your leave. Most applicants will have to schedule an interview for this, although some applicants may meet the requirements to renew past permits. The information could contain instructions specific to the place regarding scheduling your interviews, presenting your application, and other frequently asked questions. You must present (bring with you) the Confirmation and the following documents throughout the process. You will also be able to provide additional supporting documents that you consider important during your interview.*

The second page clarifies the documents you must present. *No more and no less than this very Confirmation page with a bar code legible at the time of the interview. If you do not have access to a printer at this time, choose the option of sending your Confirmation by email to a specified email address. You may print or email your Confirmation to an email address. You may print or email your application for your own records. You do NOT need to present the application at the time of the interview. Bear in mind that you could be required to provide proof that you have paid the processing fee and/or other payments related to the process. We ask that you check the Reciprocity Table for the country you are visiting to learn what other charges you may have pending. If you have additional questions or need to know how to contact our office, please see.*

On this same page—the second—another explanatory note: *Unless you are exempt from the interview, you are asked to personally sign your own application biometrically. By giving this particular kind of signature, you certify under oath that you have read and understood the questions on your application, and moreover that you yourself have made all statements truthfully and according to your best understanding and conviction.* (Understanding and conviction are repeated a couple times more in the same paragraph).

And it ends with: *The information you have provided in this application can be accessed by other agencies with the legal and statutory authority to use said information, including for law enforcement and other purposes. The photograph you have provided with your application can be used to verify your information.*

Likewise attached to this Confirmation was a letter that the Ministry sent from its Processing Center to the Department of Interests on March twentieth. In the letter, I read that the Ministry sent its greetings to the Honorable Department, grateful for its cooperation with regard to the application prepared on my behalf, bearer of ordinary number B908863. Then it explained the purpose of my application, the length of my stay, my departure and return dates. The Ministry took this opportunity to reiterate its opinion to the Department. Finally, the Ministry's stamp, no signature.

When I left the Office I went straight to my institution, first collecting my bag, then my telephone. I couldn't manage to fake a smile. I needed an explanation. "You shouldn't have gone there looking like that," they told me. "Nonsense," I retorted. "They could only see my face, maybe my shoulders and chest, through the window." "Of course they could see you. They're watching you from the moment you turn the corner; they're watching you in the park; they're watching if you talk to someone, or you sit down, or you buy a cheese sandwich, or you open your parasol. They see everything. You're so naive."

I waited a week, two weeks, three, for some sign, a call from the Ministry that would inform me about my case. Whether things had been cleared up, whether my application would be accepted—maybe not now, right away, but in the future. A layer of dust settled over the phone, and I brushed it off every night before cooking.

Many times I wished I could see that man again, the one who'd sat down next to me in the Office and with whom I'd felt so at ease. Sometimes I thought I passed him in the street, or saw him on a bus, or on some TV news report about the changes the Ministry was enacting in the country. The Office never appears on TV. Sometimes the announcers give official readings of the new laws regarding the Office. The people are distressed. The work day is affected. The institutions try to encourage discipline.

I also asked myself questions for which I would later reproach myself, branding myself ungrateful or nonconformist. They were questions no one would answer, except maybe an ingrate or a nonconformist.

I knew of several others like me, people who suffered the same fate, and of others, endorsed by an institution, who reported to the Office with applications like mine, attesting to their situations, and who were accepted, their permits granted, and who left. I don't miss those people because I only saw them in meetings, or at commemorations.

A French bulldog
and a telephone
cost the same,
and both can provide you with
the affection
you lack.

POEM

By my side you don't know what's inside me, mami. What it is to yearn to open your arms without arms, even more to open your legs without legs, or to open your chest, mami, your heart. By my side you won't be able to have a garden with those flowers, the yellow or orange ones you like so much. Or have books of poetry, academic essays, those erotic novels you like. No books, mami, none at all. By my side you won't be able to have a cat, mami, not a boy or a girl cat. No smoking, mamita, not that cigarette or the other stuff. By my side, strangely, you'll have only a little of me.

Don't say you love me, mamita, you have no idea that I'm impossible to love, to adore, or feel a certain affection for. Attachments, like asthma, suffocate me. You better go, mamita, down that road or the other one further on. Hand me the inhaler and get going. Before you go, mamita, hand me the inhaler.

When you come back, bring me something chocolate. Candy, gum, egg yolk nougat, almond nougat, dried fruit. Chocolate is bad, mami. You'll kill me with that stuff, you're going to choke me. I'll devour it. I'll lick it, suck it, and I'll nibble the corners. If you want half tell me now, because it's running out. Everything runs out, mamita. The good stuff is the first to run out. Chocolate, coffee, money, toilet paper, desire, imagination, youth, winter. It all runs out.

I have a proposal for you, mami. It's quite simple and innocent. It has to do more with you than with me, mamita, but I'm embarrassed to tell you. It has to do with something I've got that you want, and I can give it to you, mamita, if you swear to me that I'll never, ever see you again. I'll give you what you want for twenty-four hours straight, nice and open and clean, fresh out of the box for you. Only if you swear I'll never see you again.

* * *

It's a sickness, mamita, this whole situation and any other similar situation. The history of our inability to be alone, to be happy with ourselves. The need to be heard and what's worse, to listen to the other person, mami, to hear a bunch of foreign, inconsequential words. You are an individual and I am an individual, and that word, mamita, comes from a primary word that means: *a thing that cannot be divided*. The reference is simple, an independent unit, an elemental unit in a larger, more complex system, a numerically singular thing. I think it's fascinating, mami. I am fascinated.

Last night I missed you. I admit it, mami. You set a trap and I fell into it. You called me on the phone and told me you'd come by in half an hour to see me and kiss me, to give me what was mine. That's how you operate, mamita, you spend your time engaging the word NECESSITY. Because if someone needs something, that is, precisely, what belongs to them. The equation is as follows, I need it because it belongs to me. And vice versa, mami. So I missed you. I cooked for you. I put together a wonderful dish using sliced and sautéed ingredients. I showered and soaped and dried myself, for you, mamita, who never came. I laid down naked, on the sheet that *you* put on, mami, fifteen days ago. I have to wash the sheets.

At five in the morning I opened an eye, mami, and then another eye, and then my mouth. I was drowning. I always dream I'm drowning in the ocean when I have an asthma attack in my sleep. This time was no different. I was sinking and I couldn't move my arms, mamita, or my legs. It's horrible, mami, you know it is. You've seen me wake up in the middle of the night, gasping and wet. I'm all the way down there while my respiratory system is paralyzed by the contraction of my bronchial tubes. I compare my bronchial tubes to dead fish. The ocean's dead fish and my bronchial tubes lure me down, bewitching me.

Today my head hurts. It must be the heat, mami. Even the computer has been corrupted. I have zits on my neck and armpits. My hair is falling out, mami. Soon I'll be bald and people will think I'm in chemo. I don't know why everyone likes bald women. I think they find them sexy, somehow. Some kind of morbid interest related to pain or death. I'll be a sexy girl for the first time ever, mami, you'll see.

The day you disappear will be a normal day, for you as well as for me. It'll pass unceremoniously, both for you and for me. You'll get many things back, mami, things you've lost. Things that you don't even remember, that you don't recognize anymore. Meanwhile, mamita, I'll gain space and time, my whole life will be only mine, as it should be, mami, and always will be. I'll be alive again inside myself, while outside of me I'll be a bratty child climbing over rooftops. I'll buy rum in bulk and raise a glass to you on the rooftops, mami.

The best memory I'll have of you, mami, if you'll allow me, will be the way you cleaned my fan. You took it apart mechanically. You got a wet cloth. First the blades and then the motor. You got a toothbrush, and with the toothbrush you cleaned every one of the casing's plastic divisions. You stuck the toothbrush in and out around fifteen hundred times. You did it with a jeweler's care, mami, a beautiful job. I thanked you, mamita, with love. The best memory you'll have of me, you'll take with you.

We were irresponsible, mamita. We shouldn't have planned what we planned. A child, at this stage in the game, maybe a daughter. You wanted to name her Esperanza and I wanted to name her Alegría—hope or joy. Names that were too strange, mami, too exotic for our reality. Too romantic. I don't like to play with human weaknesses. For a woman, mamita, having children is essential. I don't like to play with anyone. I like to play alone. And dance alone within four walls.

You wanted me to tell you what I feel for you, mamita. What I feel for you is the same thing I feel for anyone. It's pity, nostalgia, and boredom. Things that, to tell the truth, don't mean anything. But you wanted to know, mami, so I whispered it in your ear. And now I'm repeating it so you won't forget. Because everything is forgotten. The bad stuff is the first to be forgotten. Every time you leave, mami, every time you go out that door and I'm left here dancing alone, I forget you. I forget you exist, mami. I forget what is there inside me.

What's there inside me I'm not going to tell you because it's the only thing that's mine. It's the only thing people have, their insides. It's ugly to say, mami, but I don't care about your insides. What you have inside that you always want to give me, that you offer like a gift, it slides right off me, mami. I don't want anything from you, mamita, or from anyone. I want you to leave, get on, on a plane, go far away. Whether you're happy or not doesn't matter to me either, mami. I only want you to leave and not bother me anymore with that tenderness and warmth, mami, that make me wilt.

Whether you take Air France, or Iberia Airlines, or Mexicana, or whatever other airline, doesn't matter to me either, mami.

If the flight's delayed, I'll keep you company. If you have a lot of luggage, I'll carry your luggage. If you need money, I'll borrow it, mami. We'll go to a restaurant and eat like two kings. Like two presidents. Like gods. You can wipe my mouth with your napkin, mami. You can do what you want. If the plane crashes, even better.

Nuclear family
in decline
composed
of a person
and a pet.
They seem content,
healthy.

NO ONE

ETECSA announces: Top-ups from abroad starting at twenty dollars, and domestic phone cards for twenty dollars, will give you double what you paid for between December twenty-sixth and twenty-ninth—happy new year.

Sometimes, from the highway, I can see her. I watch her for a couple of minutes, entranced by what I see; I leave the park, leave my orbit, the universal axis. Then I turn on my phone and take a poor four hundred KB photo. There's a buttress, a brick wall, that separates her from the world. Protects her from the world. Strengthens her.

* * *

The day of my thirtieth birthday I receive an empty, anony-
mous message. That same day I receive a message from my
best friend, in Toronto or Montreal, I'm not sure, saying this:
*I'm at H&M but there's practically nothing here. Do you want
a gray sweater with two black hearts?* I do want it, but I don't
have data to reply and tell him that I want it, so I sit there
thinking about my own heart, empty and black.

I'm sitting on the bed in the lotus position. Along the petal
edges and the stem, the remnants of morning dew are still visible.
Through the window a wind enters and shakes my petals violently, they fall to the floor, a cat plays with them. Not the stem.
The stem stays vertical. As you can see, Mom, your daughter is
adult enough not to care about the wind that comes in through
the window, or about the cats that appear and disappear.

I'm sitting on the bed in the downward dog position.
There is no wind coming through the window nor remnants
of morning dew. I was shaken violently, but not today. Nothing falls to the floor. Even so, I remain vertical. As you can
see, Mom, your daughter is adult enough to care about the
things that really warrant it. What opinion do I warrant from
you, if someone were ever to ask?

*   *   *

While I watch her, enormous as a tree, I ignore the rust. She is rusty and her paint is peeling, like all of her kind, but she is still beautiful. I would venture to swear that she is the only beautiful thing in the city. The only thing worth seeing in terms of tourism, for example. A tourism based on estrangement, of course. An intelligent tourism.

It's important to me to think of you with a poem in your eyes today. With water in your hands. I wish you a new year full of days and places that are beautiful. True things.

From a city called Havana to an almost rural town called Camagüey—an aboriginal name, very sonorous. The last time I made this trip I did it with my temple resting on your thighs. The bus crosses the bridge over the Zaza River at one forty-four in the morning. At eighty-five kilometers per hour. In the river at that hour, things are not the same. What lives there most certainly has another state that it will lose at dawn. Seat number one of the bus is for me, a river mighty and black that has no outlet. Entertained by my thoughts, I see the digital clock above the driver flash one fifty-three.

In the span of nine minutes I believe I've interpreted life and death. But once again, I've understood it wrong.

ETECSA announces: Someone misses you so much they could become athingthatdoesnotexist until they are back in your arms again.

Before midnight I receive the longed for top-up, twenty dollars doubled that will become many minutes of happiness and that I'll have to mete out with utter sobriety, with impartial care. Before midnight, as well, the various states of mind intensify, the estrangement, terror, euphoria. Situations quite opposed to impartiality. It's comforting when the terror gives way to euphoria and then to tacit sleep, even if only for four hours. Before the four hours are up, I hear a voice in the Nokia Lumia that is ever less familiar. It's been nearly three months.

My opinion of highways is without a doubt a cliché and one of the most commonplace platitudes in the whole field of architecture. Highways are monotonous, and when traveling on them from one set of coordinates to another, a person remains the same. And that's why I harbor no compassion or affinity for highways, almost always adorned with signage of a political or educational nature, and instead I reject and avoid them, especially if the trip is a return. A return—another atrocious cliché—should not be undertaken on a highway.

For a while now I've seen that she has company. The wall isn't so high, and if I'm on foot nothing stops me from standing on tiptoe. A double has been placed in front of her and it looks as though they are talking; she leans over, the other does too, in mutual complicity. Ultimately, though my interpretation of reality differs, they are nothing but simple tools, not even intelligent machines. Me, I'm neither simple nor intelligent, though sometimes I'm a little of both. I peer over, turn on the phone, take a poor four hundred KB photo; I print it at a PhotoService for twenty-five cents, tape it to the refrigerator door. A double is placed in front of me, it opens the refrigerator door, and thinks, *There's nothing here, either.*

It's the end of the year on an island and it's assumed, like every day and at the end of every year, that one should open the refrigerator and take something out. I open it and take out a can of beer that's been frozen since the year two thousand four, when the island's president tripped and fell after giving a speech and was sick like an animal, like a man. The beer froze without us realizing, it went bad, it busted, it died, it disappeared. I hate the end as much as the beginning. I hate you. Give me that. Give me that, or I'll take this beer and give it to you in your face until I break your nose. An island is violence.

I understand that I'll arrive and I'll start to work in whatever turns up: a corner shop, an old folks' home, a cash register, a sink, a stoplight. I understand this but I don't practice for it, and I know it's an understanding I should rehearse for ahead of time, essay out with hands and feet, with eyes fixed intently on an imaginary point. A written essay wouldn't work, for obvious reasons. It's full-on thirty-first, right at midnight. I go outside holding a suitcase to take a turn around the block. To attract the idea of the journey and, above all, the journey itself. A journey to the future. Something I have never done or even rehearsed, and it turns out to be a good walk, just a little dust between my toes thanks to the flip-flops, and two or three scratches from the rocks, the barbed wire. A drunk crosses my path. The suitcase wheels don't acknowledge him.

Three streets further on, parallel to my street, always stood the building where she lived—a woman I've known since I was sixteen, the first to embarrass me with a simple question I answered in the negative. The question was: *Do you know how to play?* The woman, then a kid six months younger than me, started moving the pieces by herself on the unfamiliar board. She moved black and white and filled me with envy of both kinds, malicious and benign, and she checkmated herself, looking at me out of the corner of her eye to accentuate the humiliation. I hated her from my darkest depths, and I loved her just as deeply. Now she is in front of me, asking me another question that I've forbidden myself to answer. Answers in the affirmative are always the most dangerous.

The authors I've been reading lately alternate between Czech and Austrian nationalities, so I can get this off my chest, off my head, off my belly, I can let it fall on my foot so the nail on my big toe falls off, because I know that the character or characters to imitate will not be silly psychologies but quite the opposite, consummate constructions from consummate literatures from consummate authors, the whole deal. With this generalization in mind I've lost all interest in the Latin Americans, the North Americans, the Asians, and the

Africans. I know, of course, that I'm committing a grave mistake. I will try to correct it in the coming years. It isn't wisdom that I need.

They call them brindles, those dogs whose fur recalls a tiger or a kind of badly colored cat. Likewise, brindle, I'm going now to Western Union, an agency that offers strange services to the population. Likewise, brindle, I'm going now to Transtur, a travel agency that offers three main ticket options, differentiated by cost and length of stay. Likewise, brindle, I put one foot on the landing strip, the border; I address the first official I see and I ask for asylum, I want to conform, I am nonconforming. The official's fur, sticking out above his ears without conforming to the official hat, recalls a tiger or a kind of badly colored cat.

The worst part of being no one is not exactly, as logic would have it—assuming it is logical to be someone—being no one, but rather knowing, and on top of that accepting, that you are no one here and now. The phenomenon happens all the time, in any society and in any system—one or the other will harbor the individual and at the same time throw him out, in this eternal circle that at times doesn't even suffer movement. To posit a straight line as a universe, a core, an individual, a heart, in the twenty-first century, winter of two thousand fifteen, would be an optimistic and of course naive cliché. However, to posit a straight line as a classical symphony or an electrocardiogram is without a doubt a better represented idea of anxiety, though not logical.

There is only one way to know that you are alone, believing you are not.

I need an array of elements in order to believe I am OK. And the same number of elements to believe the opposite. I need to share in order to lose, and to know in order to scorn. The place *is*. In spite of its coordinate and circumstance. Not the circumstance of water on all sides, but, in perpetual contradiction, the circumstance of the desert (hunger and filth) on all sides, confronting the circumstance of appearance (family and filth) on all sides. Testimony and chronicle of reality, the west exists on the screen. It is a document and a misleading, painful question. It can be heard and seen, but not touched. I touched it.

It's wrong because there are no horses. Western movies start with a horse, then there's a man, then a bottle, then a snake, then a cactus, then a whistle. Then another man with his bottle, his snake, his cactus, and his whistle. That's to say the adversaries, or the friends, or the lovers. But it's all wrong because the main thing, the horse, is missing. Or someone wanted to play a dirty trick and removed the horse from the scene. Because if you look at it from the angle of signs, ethically and aesthetically, the rest of the elements can be easily taken away. Man, bottle, snake, cactus, whistle. Take away the horse (beauty and work), and we're left with five heroic elements that in the west are the most ruthless and common of commonplaces.

It's also wrong because there's no love, either. Or hate. Western movies sweat love and hate from their pores, all the time, from the opening credits to the closing ones. If I say that there is love and there is hate, where are they?

The truth, being relative, outdoes and underestimates itself. North and south, east and west, up and down. Men and women, children and old people in the interminable west that, when captured by an insomniac and intelligent eye, becomes truth. Not the truth about which one says, "Yes, that's true," but the kind one only looks down at with a slight shake of the head, or maybe says: "No, that's true." This affirmation/negation constitutes the foundation of a truth, and for me it could be the greatest truth in the world, the most enchanting hoax, and the only thing that matters in the field of indiscipline. Yes, this is the west, I live here. I know what's happening.

On opening a book and starting—not starting to open it but rather to read it—something happens. My notion of the day-to-day changes, and my obligations to it become less than weak in the face of the new tasks imposed on me.

ETECSA is a phone company involved in various processes, including some natural ones. In its manual, there are no blank pages. Only regular pages, and yellow ones. Promotions for top-ups from abroad happen at the end of the month, but you can't get used to that.

On preferring
the cheese croissant,
my French bulldog
demonstrates to me,
in the first place,
that he has
very good taste,
and in the second,
that he will be very hard
to please.

PLASTIC

If I were a man more or less fifty years old, my life would surely go like this:

Before going into the house, I park the car in the garage. The house cost me forty thousand, and that was with nothing in it, just some wiring and the water tank. It was a sacrifice, but I'll be compensated down the road. My daughters are happy. The dog comes to greet me. My wife has the table set when I arrive. They would have liked to buy a house closer to the city, but the city is a monster, and we can take the car there anytime.

First, my older daughter and I moved in. Then my wife

and my younger daughter. The dog came on an in-between trip, because the girls love him. He's a street dog we found years ago. We took him in, cared for him, cleaned him up, and these days it could be said he is the best dog we've ever had.

The girls call me papi. My wife calls me papi. I'm sure that, every time he opens his mouth and barks affectionately at me, the dog is calling me papi. So that's my name. First and last.

I was born on September eleventh, nineteen seventy-three, in an unpopulated region; I was given ID number seventy-three-oh-nine, eleven-oh-nine, one-twenty-nine; married, working-class background. My driver's license number is the same as my ID number.

Our house is situated to the east of the city. The place is calm, silent, though in times of crisis we can get break-ins, assaults, even murders.

Before looking at my email, once I'm sitting in my office with the air sufficiently cooled, I take a plastic bag I've crumpled up and turned into a ping-pong ball, and I throw it into the waste-basket. I never miss. From my chair to the basket it's about three meters and change. The plastic bag traces a more or less perfect parabola. In my inbox, seventeen new messages that I must read carefully, interpret, answer. The plastic bag in the garbage uncrumples in slow motion.

And if I were a serious, stoic, and clever man, my life would surely go like this, or maybe not:

Every day I drive through the tunnel and travel a rectilinear course down one of the city's main avenues, relaxing and delighting in the trees, elegantly pruned and precisely distributed. The cleanliness of this area, with its shopping complexes, its embassies and private companies, attests to a better world, a natural order.

I can see the particles of oxygen flying around a line of cars, all gray and in perfect running condition, just as every one of us men who work here deserve. I observe the friendliness of these men as they let the next guy pass, because they forgot something in their offices and have to turn around. I imagine how hot it must be outside and I give thanks for my vehicle, equipped with an adjustable temperature that makes me smile and drive simultaneously. Sometimes, I even have erections of happiness before entering the tunnel, and once I'm inside, surrounded by the lights of other cars that have also entered the darkness, I ejaculate fleetingly into a plastic bag that I always carry with me for these occasions. The other drivers, perhaps, are happy with life like I am.

Before parking the car, I have vexing thoughts. I see my daughters from the car and I don't recognize them. They were so little when they were born. Now they're big and wide, and each of them has a voice with a different lilt, each has a different way of looking at me, a different way of obeying me. Sometimes they talk to me without looking at me. They say papi and I know that's me, but it's not me they're looking at. I love them a lot and I also love my wife. I worry about their needs and I caress my wife, but maybe they don't need my love. Maybe they need another kind of love. Something else.

Lying in bed, I turn my head and I don't know if this woman is my wife. She calls me papi and I know that's me and in the darkness I touch her, I satisfy her, but I'm not sure she is the same woman I married. She has shrunk, narrowed. Sometimes I don't fit inside her. I don't desire her. Maybe she doesn't desire me, either. I prefer to read and go quickly to sleep. She reads all the time. The news.

If I were, moreover, a man who took advantage of every opportunity that presented itself, this would be the course of a spiraling parabola:

My political trajectory, starting at twenty-six years old, has only taken place in intimate, ultra-secret circles. During the Battle of Ideas I supplied ideas, domestic products.

Before turning left to head straight home, I stop at a non-state cafe where they sell various pastries of different prices, sizes, and flavors. I order a caramel pastry, a lemon one, and a chocolate one. It's Friday and I like to pamper my family. Even the dog will get a taste of each of the pastries I've bought. Pastries and white cheese. White cheese and olives. Olives and butter. Butter and bread. Bread and ham. Ham and spinach croquettes. Spinach croquettes and plain yogurt. Plain yogurt and small servings of apricot.

I predict that my wife will choose the lemon pastry, my older daughter will like the caramel pastry, and the youngest will stick her little fingers into the chocolate. Unwittingly, when I think about my daughter's little fingers, I experience another erection. I place the pastry boxes to one side, start the car, unfold another plastic bag. Now it's distasteful.

As a buyer/seller, which is my current profession, I am in charge of overseeing consignment at certain branches of a State Company, and I've achieved a significant increase in sales over these three years of work. In two thousand eleven, sales came to four point six billion pesos. In two thousand twelve, there were six point five billion. In two thousand thirteen and through the first half of two thousand fourteen, billing is up to eight point five billion pesos. A record that weighs on my shoulders. Weighs like my daughters' futures and the well-being I've promised to my wife.

The promises a man makes should be kept to a T. In his work, as well, a man should fulfill his duties. And if he's someone like me, who buys and sells highly valued products, he should bear in mind specifications, general selling conditions, or the result will be catastrophic.

For example, I always keep orders in mind. They must be processed in writing, by fax, or by email, indicating code and quantity. The quantity should match the containers indicated in the price. Conditions or clauses included in the customers' requests will not be allowed except by prior agreement. And most important of all: for custom products, no orders will be accepted without first sending samples. Payment must be made within ninety days, and it must be received in-house. Returns or exchanges must be communicated in writing to our office for approval. Returns or exchanges will not be accepted more than fifteen days after delivery. In the case of returns for reasons not attributable to our Company, a charge will be applied for the handling and re-shelving of the merchandise. Our Company reserves the right to vary packaging and pricing.

Before the door opens I take a step back, the pastry boxes in my arms. They'll come running to me like a herd, they will hug me and kiss me, they'll say, Yum, papi, those look good! I take a step back, and another step, and another. I go back to the car. I'm careful not to make noise. The dog must be asleep because he didn't hear me pull up, didn't bark, didn't wag his tail, didn't say papi's home. I back up very slowly; tires make noise, the grass crunches, I am careful.

Back on the highway, I try to remember. The last time I bought plastic bags was three days ago. I can't go anywhere like that, without at least a dozen bags. I park the car in front of a gas station. I go into the little market where one can secure the bare minimum of necessities, like soap, toilet paper, spaghetti, plastic bags. I order a coffee and sit down. Six damp arms, covered in sweat, hug my back, shoulders, and chest. Papi, what are you doing here?

But I'm not a man, I'm not even forty years old yet. I like to laugh loud and hard even if I have bits of croissant between my teeth, and I understand nothing about buying and selling.

My best friend
found a cat
and named it Wanda.
It had a penis
and testicles,
and she named it Wanda.

WANDA

My husband and I were teenage sweethearts.
The house where we lived had only one floor.
We built the second floor ourselves.
Hand over hand and brick over brick.
With a spiral staircase.
The whole town was jealous of the staircase.
And we painted it red.
The color of passion.

I got pregnant right away.

First the boy and then the girl.

My husband wanted the perfect pair.

And we had the perfect pair.

And I birthed them both at home because there wasn't time
to take me into the city.

My husband got drunk and fell into a ditch, both times.

And there was no time to take me.

Both times I pushed, like a woman, and the kids came out.

The boy looks like me and the girl looks like him.

It's always like that, apparently.

A matter of genetics.

Twenty years we've been together.

Both a civil and a church ceremony.

The whole town was jealous when we had a church
wedding.

They're not even that Christian, they said.

They don't even believe in God that much, they said.

God forgive them.

And keep them.

My husband's father lives a block away from us.

He was widowed four years ago and hasn't been with
   anyone since.
He goes out dirty and talks to himself.
I go over to visit him.
I bring him a little soup, if I make soup.
Or a little chicken and rice, if I make chicken and rice.
The kids went to see him at first.
Now they go less and less.
They're afraid of him.
In town they say he has a shotgun.

My husband isn't the same anymore.
I'm not the same, either.
I've realized that, but he hasn't.
And I'm tired.
Two months ago, I told him to get out.
He fought it, but in the end he left.
He put everything into a bag, his clothes and tools, and he
   left.
An entire life.
He didn't go to his father's house, but to a friend's.
It's better that way, he can talk with someone his own age.
The kids fought it too.

They wanted to go with him.
Kids are like that.

My girlfriends gave me a lot of support.
If you don't love him anymore, you have to leave him, they
    said.
If you don't love him, you can't pretend.
We're behind you, they said.
My boss really supported me, too.
He's a very attentive man.
Last month, he brought me a black prince bud.
A flower for a flower, was his phrase.
My girlfriends filled a glass with water so I could put the
    black prince in it.

Last week, my boss spent the night with me.
The kids went to their grandfather's.
They spent the night there.
They were annoyed with me.
They didn't speak to me for two days.
Kids are like that.
My boss treats me like a queen.

This morning I arrived at work and found a flower on my
 desk.
A black prince.
I can't imagine how he did it, because we left the
 house together.
I hugged him and gave him a kiss on the forehead, my love.
What a sweetheart you are, he told me.
You're the sweetheart, I said.
When are you going to get divorced? he asked.
Don't pressure me, I said.

At ten in the morning, my girlfriends went to buy coffee.
I stayed behind to make some headway.
There are so many reports to turn in.
And stamp.
I'm going crazy here.
I looked at the black prince and sighed.
How many petals does a rose have?
The doorbell rang.
Too soon for it to be my friends and the coffee.

It was my husband with a machete.
Get out of here.

I'm not leaving.

I said get out.

I'm not leaving.

OK then, what do you have to say?

Nothing.

Then what do you want?

To kill you, whore.

Your mother's the whore.

My mother's dead, whore.

Then your aunt.

I'll cut off your hands, that'll teach you.

They'll arrest you if you do.

What do I care?

Look, you'd better go.

He brought the machete down on one arm, then the other.

My hands fell at the feet of the desk.

The black prince trembled.

I went outside bleeding, and my husband was still there.

No one came out to defend me, they were all so jealous.

Now you'll see, whore.

He stuck the machete into my stomach and sliced me up to
    my throat like a pig.

So you'll learn, whore.
If you're not mine, you're no one's.
You bastard.
Asshole.

From there he went to his father's house.
He had everything prepared.
The rope hanging from the pipe.
The knot.
Everything.
He stood on the chair.
Put the rope around his neck.
He jumped and broke the pipe.
He ended up alive, on the floor, like a chicken.
Doesn't matter.

Where the hell is the shotgun?
He searched the whole house for the shotgun.
He opened the fridge.
Drank some water.
The only thing in the fridge was water.
And vinegar.
The shotgun was behind the bedroom door.

Covered in dust.
He brushed it off.
Fired.
Perfect.

That was when my friends returned.
With a little coffee in a plastic cup.
Cold coffee.
Old.
And half a pizza.
Cheese pizza.
Colder than a dead man's toe.

My mother was outside the morgue.
My daughter was there.
My husband's father was there.
And some neighbors and the police.
The boy didn't come because he was ashamed.
Boys are like that.
They don't understand.

My husband's father and the neighbors wanted to have the

wake for both of us.
In our house.
With my children, the family, and the neighbors.
And my mother was against it.
He killed her, goddammit.
Because he loved her so much.
But he killed her, goddammit.
Because he loved her so much.
Go hold his wake in hell.

In the end the wake was for both of us.
Upstairs in the bedroom.
One coffin beside the other.
The whole town went up the spiral staircase.
These stairs are such a pretty red, they said.
They came up to pay their respects.
They only stayed a little while.

My boss came upstairs too.
He asked my mother for permission to put a black prince in
my coffin.
My husband's father stood up and went out for some fresh
air.

Maybe he thought it was indecent.

Or that he'd have to find a black prince for his son.

My mother gave him permission.

The kids didn't.

They were very elegant, sitting beside the coffins.

But they didn't want to see any black princes anywhere.

No flowers.

Kids are like that.

I sleep.
I can't breathe.
I choke on water.
At the bottom
of the ocean
there's a Samsung
Galaxy
vibrating.

GOD

Mom said, "Take care of each other and respect each other. She said, "Respect each other a lot, and take care of each other." She said it once a day at first, then twice, then three times, and so on, until the thing became a symphony.

But *she* would come in, look at me, sit down, look at me, open her legs, look at me, pick up the contraption, look at me, put it between her legs, look at me, settle it in, look at me, adjust the endpin, look at me, turn the pegs, look at me, tighten the strings, look at me. She looked at me the same way Mom did, with the same chin, the same nose, the same teeth.

Mom had perfect teeth, and she wanted us to take care of each other. Take care of each other like sisters do. But she looked at me with the same eyes as Mom. Mom went to a mission.

The whole town had been going off, little by little, to missions. People went off for years to serve in impenetrable places, catastrophic countries, sick countries, people sick in abstract organs invisible to the eye. And the whole town had been going off, little by little, to save people, strangers, they were swept up by the concept of solidarity. Solidarity turned into dollars, into food, into household appliances. Over chat, even after weeks went by, Mom said, "Take care of each other, I love you both a lot, I see you in every little girl who crosses my path."

Over chat, even after ten months, Mom said, "Don't disrespect each other, defend each other, take good care of each other, I remember you always."

Over chat, even after two years, Mom said, "Take care of each other, protect each other, think of me, don't forget me." Mom said that and most of the time she'd sit stiff in silence looking at us while we sat stiff and looked at her, and nodded, yes, that we loved each other more all the time.

In spite of the mission, the distance, and the chat, Mom's teeth were still the same.

Missionary Mom missed us, but she had to fulfill her mission, she had to have solidarity and be self-critical, she had to save the lives of other people from other towns in other jungles in other countries on other continents. And she had to return home with her hands and feet and soul full of gifts, countless gifts, for her teenage young adult grown-up elderly daughters.

That's what we were and that's what we'll continue to be. Two teenage young adult grown-up elderly girls. A couple of girls without their missionary mom in the house to yank their ears, to separate them.

So *she* would come in, look at me, sit down, look at me, open her legs, look at me, pick up the contraption, look at me, put it between her legs, look at me, settle it in, look at me, adjust the endpin, look at me, turn the pegs, look at me, tighten the strings, look at me. She looked at me the same way Mom did, with the same chin, the same nose, the same teeth. Mom had perfect teeth, and she wanted us to take care of each other. Take care of each other like sisters. But she looked at me with the same eyes as Mom. The same familial nature. An expression between seductive and mischievous. The mission of mischievousness that we had to carry out.

—Now I can't write, thanks to you.

—But I have to practice.

—Learn to practice quietly.

—The contraption doesn't play quietly, it's not electric, it doesn't have volume.

—There's no volume in your head, either.

—There's no music in your head.

—Yes there is.

—Oh yeah? What music?

—Come here.

Then she came over, closer, pretended to lift up a lid, pretended to peer into the emptiness, blew with her mouth and her teeth, which were Mom's mouth and teeth; she pretended to stick her hand into a hole, pretended to pull something out, and she started rolling with laughter.

—See, there's music.

—It's not music, dummy. What I just took out of your head is a round stone, a pebble from paradise.

—My head's not paradise.

—Your head is a music-less paradise full of pebbles, air, and fear.

—Why fear?

—You're afraid of Bach.

—What I'm afraid of is all his preludes together.
—You're afraid of Bach.

Yes. I'm afraid of Bach. I'm afraid of Mom. I'm afraid of the comandante who sent Mom to a mission. I'm afraid of *her*, the one who takes care of me and whom I take care of and who plays Bach with her legs apart, sitting on a chair with her legs apart with her chest out with her chin out with her face contorting from the sounds of Bach. Sounds that are revolutionary, solidary, syllabary. I'm afraid of the comandante who sends missionaries to abandon their daughters.

Yes. Missions Avenue, August thirteenth, twelfth meridian. Eleven missionaries parade past to celebrate the comandante's birthday, and to listen to the comandante speak, and to obey his orders. The comandante gives love and orders. The comandante needs to send them to a mission. The mission is secret. The mission is a miracle.

Yes. I'm afraid of missions. I'm afraid of reptiles. I'm afraid of Facebook. I'm afraid of chat. I'm afraid of the female mosquito. I'm afraid of food. I'm afraid of clarity. I'm afraid of money. I'm afraid of new clothes. I'm afraid of a pebble. I'm afraid of poetry. I'm afraid of music.

Yes. Las Misiones Airport where Mom left from, and where María left from, and Elvira, and Reina, and Amelia, and Cristina, and Luisa, and Susana, and Esperanza, and Flor, and Carmen, and Laura, and Sofía, and Ester, and Virginia, and Lisbet, and Liset, and Elena, and Caridad.

Yes. I'm afraid of Luigi Boccherini. I'm afraid of Gaspar Cassadó. I'm afraid of Han-Na Chang. I'm afraid of Jacqueline du Pré. I'm afraid of Emanuel Feuermann. I'm afraid of Pierre Founier. I'm afraid of Antonio Janigro. I'm afraid of Yo-Yo Ma. I'm afraid of Mischa Maisky. I'm afraid of Jacques Offenbach. I'm afraid of Carlos Prieto. I'm afraid of János Starker. I'm afraid of Paul Tortelier.

Yes. Blue sea of the missions where I dip my foot when I go to the sea and my mission is only that, to put my foot in it. My first foot and my second foot, and then she comes closer, looks at me, puts her feet in.

Yes. I'm afraid of Angola. I'm afraid of Miami. I'm afraid of Warsaw. I'm afraid of Paris. I'm afraid of Moscow. I'm afraid of Caracas. I'm afraid of Barcelona. I'm afraid of Nafpaktos. I'm afraid of Johannesburg. I'm afraid of Tokyo. I'm afraid of Jerusalem. I'm afraid of Nagasaki. I'm afraid of Port-au-Prince. I'm afraid of Tijuana. I'm afraid of Havana. I'm afraid of fear.

Yes.

Yes.

She was also a little afraid. Doctors, nurses, engineers, teachers, construction workers, peasants, everyone, had been heading off to a mission. Artists, economists, lawyers, salespeople, writers, musicians, had been heading off to a mission. At this point no one was left in the city.

No one.

No one.

She woke up in the night with a muffled scream. She called to me. She threw the contraption at me. She signaled for me to place it next to me, on my other side. She jumped from her bed to my bed like an amphibian from one rock to another. She checked to see that the contraption was well placed. She covered herself with my sheet, head and all. She curled up beside me like a damp pebble. She slept.

The rest was normal and sequential. Every night the same thing. Amphibian jump in the early morning. Shared sheet. Dampness.

In the early morning of one August thirteenth, I woke up dreaming of the comandante. It was the commemoration of the real comandante's birth—he was turning around a hundred that day. The comandante was a warm girl, at my side, who wanted to send me to a mission. To convince me that the mission was truly important and that I had to leave my house to go there, she kissed me on the mouth in an exemplary way, she put her tongue in, wrapped it around my tongue, licked my gums, cleaned my teeth, slobbered on my lips, and of course, I understood that I had to leave my house to go to a mission. Commander-in-chief, give your order.

Mom said to take good care of each other, and we really did take good care of each other, we respected each other and loved each other more all the time. Over chat I promised Mom I'd buy my sister a new apparatus, not with the money Mom sent us for food, but with my own money, a bunch of dollars that I'd won in a contest. The contest was about knowledge. The question over the radio was: Who composed the art of fugue?

I bought her a new instrument, a top-of-the-line Stradivarius, with a wheeled case so she didn't have to strain herself.

I lost my fear of Bach.

I lost my fear of the comandante.

If someone calls
and tells you no,
hang up quickly.
If someone calls
and tells you yes,
hang up quickly,
as well.

MIAMI

If I count the people my poor eyes (astigmatism and vision loss) can see in just a few minutes, maybe I'll get up to a million. In my right hand, a hundred books and in my left, my passport. The hundred books weigh more than me, so I hurry to find a cart where I can deposit the bag that holds them. I tug on the cart but I can't get it out. I pull harder and nothing. The cart backs up toward me in reverse along an aluminum rail, but it won't come off. I have to put my credit card into a slot in the wall. The slot in the wall is a machine that will access my credit, subtracting a small amount, and the cart will come off the rail. But I don't have a card. Or credit. In the place I come from, cards and credit don't exist.

WYNWOOD, THREE IN THE MORNING.

The black city sleeps. It wakes slowly, one eye, another eye, other eyes, other human beings. The buses approach in a straight line; I don't see them arrive because if I turn my face, the wind blows my hair, it's annoying. I don't even look at the cars; they upset me.

The bus brakes, stops, doesn't lose speed, gains space. It's my space. It has the look of an animal, of an immense plant. It costs a dollar, more or less, maybe two. The girl invites me to get on with a friendly gesture. I get on. Inside, everyone is black. Black old women, black men, black children, my girl. The air conditioning, cruel, makes everyone bristle. The girl caresses me, rubs my arms to warm me up. It burns. There is an imperceptible movement of my arms that denotes estrangement. I find it a little pathetic that I don't know how to detach, can't manage anything less than astonishment.

Half an hour before the bus arrived, I walked beside this girl along a sidewalk of squirrels, raccoons, flowers. Not speaking, only smiling, rushing toward the bus. Laughter replaced language, cancelling it out.

It's a bus and two women, poor, strangers.

PANTHER COFFEE, TEN IN THE MORNING.

The people are beautiful. Never in my life do I remember having seen so many beautiful people within a single perimeter, without suffocating. Inside and out, beautiful, marvelous. They speak English, Spanish, French, Portuguese, Japanese, Arabic, German. They tell the truth and they lie. They can lie because they're beautiful and they drink coffee very elegantly. They open their computers and type quickly very elegantly. They order iced teas and chew whole-grain sandwiches with even more elegance. They enjoy their appearances, they smack their lips, they smile at each other, forget what brought them precisely to this place. They enjoy life and the coffee. They buy Bolivian coffee, Colombian, Brazilian, Venezuelan, American. They're kings. They reign and order. They command and exchange. They exist.

For my part, I'm a cat, seated and calm. She's a cat too. Loose braids. Standing behind the counter. Serving them all.

She purrs toward me, a mug in her hands for me, hot. Almond milk. Heart.

I take a photo of the almond heart with my phone.

Cat and happy.

BOOKS&BOOKS, TWO IN THE AFTERNOON.

Suddenly the opposite. Grimace, glass, paper. Pricey, pricey books that I can't and don't want to read. Classics. Modern. Contemporary. Tables with umbrellas. Writers more illustrious than the books. White wine in fine glassware. Sightseers and bystanders. Three women writers sitting side by side not knowing what to say to themselves. One crosses her hands, another crosses her legs, another calls the waiter over.

Buy whatever you want, my treat.

I want to flee and collide with a tree that smells of damp resin.

We don't have trees, only books or glassware.

I want to flee and collide with a tree that smells of damp resin.

A FRIEND'S HOUSE, NINE AT NIGHT.

Six of us girls are sharing a platter. There's a lot. Colors and flavors unknown until now. One friend takes a roll and puts it in my mouth. "This won't make you fat." Another friend takes a roll and puts it in my mouth. "It doesn't make you fat or nourish you." So the taste is still unknown. I only see the rolls go straight into my mouth, I don't know what they taste like.

We're too sober. Bored and sober. Playing at sticking random things in our mouths. Sensual. Hungerless. We have to eat it all.

It's sushi and it's Japanese.

"You want a gin and tonic?"

I like my friends and the foreign warmth, things foreign to reality. I like to sweat and get nervous. I like beer and plastic, canned vegetables. Everything rots so easily here.

My girlfriends smoke like chimneys. They go outside to smoke. They're the prettiest chimneys I know.

I like everything with my friends. Without them, the city is a giant hormone, speaking to me in English and Spanish at the same time.

I'm in love.

Listen here.

With you all.

Later I laugh with other friends through a screen. I cover a thousand latitudes in half an hour, skirting a digital country that, tired as I get, never ends.

DOLPHIN MALL, MID-MORNING.

A little like an airport, but without the need to get anywhere.

Buy. Buy. Buy.

Forever 21, underwear.

Aéropostale, a shirt.

Gap, a dress and a pair of shorts.

Chocolate. Stairs. Lights.

Android.

Transgender.

Triumph.

Bienvenido al paradise.

Sit down and breathe.

You're in control.

JOSÉ KOZER'S HOUSE, NOON.

Before me a famous man who gives me the shivers. He's tall. He's a tree. He's a beautiful monster with branches. Instead of two hands he has three hands. Long. Luminous. His fingernail beds measure two centimeters. I always notice the size of fingernails. Fingers and nails inspire pleasure in me, excitement.

His wife, the same. A beautiful monster with branches. Green branches. Green flowers, too.

They take turns talking. My ovaries hurt. I go to the bathroom several times. I expel blood, urine, gases.

She makes raw fish, with lemon and basil and herbs that I cannot enjoy.

I chew looking at the man, who talks about poetry and money at the same time.

Speak nature.

Speak palm, pine.

I've been waiting for you for a while.

TATTOO STUDIO, SEVEN THIRTY IN THE EVENING.

My friend picks me up in her car, bought on credit and used, comfortable. I get into the car. I look out the window as I ride. Highway. Cars. I get dizzy. She knows where we're going, but I don't. It's her goodbye present. A promise. I look at her from my seat beside her. She's five years younger than me. I like her a lot. She attracts me like a movie on the big screen starring my favorite actors and actresses. I need to have an accident.

She works at a bank and because of that she says we have nothing in common. She kisses me. She holds me against her chest. She says I'm so little. They all say the same thing. What a drag. When she brushes my buttocks by accident, she startles and looks deeply into my eyes, her lips half-open, her eyes watery. Maybe I'm imagining it. I want to marry her.

We go into the tattoo and piercing studio. The adrenaline rises. I love tattoos and piercings, although I would never get a tattoo or a piercing on my genitals. The idea is terrifying.

I want to get my nose pierced. Through the septum so I'll look like a cow, but I won't moo, or eat dry grass, or bathe in a lake on the outskirts of town. I'll take the bull by the horns, till the cows come home.

A piercing is a hoop, with two little steel balls that screw onto the ends. Very delicate, and feminine.

The piercer is a sad Peruvian woman with the expression of one who hasn't had sex in many days, or eaten anything tasty in many days, or seen an astonishing movie, or laid eyes on the ocean.

The Peruvian woman grabs my septum with scissors that have a hole on either side, and it hurts. I close my eyes. Open them. I tell her to show me the rest of her tools. She shows me.

"If you don't want to, don't."

"I want to."

My friend gives me her hand. My hand in her hand makes me decide to do it; I'm brave.

The Peruvian woman puts a metal bar through the circular ends of the scissors, and then through that she'll introduce the piercing, in the form of a hoop. I want to. Cold-blooded. The pressure of the Peruvian's hands is in harmony with hatred and revenge. It hurts more than a tattoo, more than love.

I expel blood, tears, mucus. It all mixes and drips down. My friend laughs. I laugh and cry.

The piercing looks as though it's always been there. Since my birth.

I thank the Peruvian.

The Peruvian thanks me.

Forty dollars.

INTERNET, MIDNIGHT.

Since I've been here, I click on the Wi-Fi icon and connect. Where I live there is no such thing as Wi-Fi. My best friend lives in Canada. My sister lives in Tenerife. My dad lives on a lost island. My exes live in Mexico, Brazil, and New York. And so on, successively. A mule train of people I never imagined living without. Those people are there, connected every day, present. Now I, too, am present. I also have a name and a profile, and a status I can update every day. I see them. I hear them. They're desperate, want to catch up. We cry together, as a group. We go to bed and get up together. We well know it has an end.

I love you.

Me too.

Good night.

See you tomorrow.

FAREWELL PARTY, TIMELESS.

It starts with "Fast Car," by Tracy Chapman. It ends with a song I don't remember. Not because I don't remember, but because some people have vomited, others are talking, and others, like she and I, are dancing strangely in the kitchen, her lips in front of my lips, a few millimeters away. Our respirations are very close to each other.

My arms don't take her by the waist, her arms don't hold me. It's a state of freedom and pleasure reached very few times in our lives, like a song.

At the party we had beers, cocktails, gin and tonic, marihuana, mushrooms, fish, meat, vegetables, barbecue, hummus.

We had everything.

We had what we deserved.

I don't remember the last song.

AIRPORT, EIGHT IN THE MORNING.

The name of the airline isn't well known. Once I'm back home I'll forget it. Same as the unpleasant experiences.

We arrive, weigh the suitcases, wrap them in plastic to hold them tight and protect them. We check in, pay. The people who've been in charge of me stay with me until after four in the afternoon. I thank them. I thank them infinitely. They are not kindred souls. I seem strange and ungrateful to them. Careless, awkward. They expected something else from me. I wasn't expecting anything from them.

The flight has been delayed because there are problems with the plane. They buy me water, food. They hug me coldly. I try to look them in the eyes and transmit connection. They avoid my gaze. Our eyes don't meet. They leave.

I sit glued to my phone, talking to my friends, waiting for a sign to appear. The sign doesn't appear.

Twenty-four hours later they announce the plane's departure. They lead us down a hall to gate number so-and-so. We have the right to potato chips, hamburgers, apples, soft drinks. Airline's treat. I don't take anything.

Sunscreen
on your hands
and on your chest.
You know a
woman's true age
by looking there.

CLITORIS

I reported my situation on a Monday morning. I did it duly, in writing, to the Clinic. On Wednesday they called me in. The doctor lifted my skirt, separated the hair a little, and observed the irritation with the expression of a scientist. She put on gloves and took out a medicated cream. She spread the cream over my genitals and looked at me again the same way. A way of looking with a penetrating gaze, raising her eyebrows, opening her eyes nice and wide. She didn't even cover her mouth. I reached the lodging with its sixty beds and threw myself on mine. My body resounded on the batting like a sack of rice when it's dropped. The Clinic was a horrible place. Silent and white, but horrible. The doctors who worked there gave the impression they were veterinarians.

The next morning I was worse. The cream the doctor had applied was still there, sticky; my skin hadn't absorbed it. I couldn't open my legs. It hurt as much as it burned. I headed to the phones to call Mom. Girls from my class were sitting in front of the phones. When they saw me they started to laugh. They laughed in loud peals, pointed their fingers at my legs, covered their noses. They wanted me to cry and I obliged, ashamed. Mom answered the phone a few seconds later. I asked her to come pick me up. To save me. I explained my situation to her. The urgency of the situation. She promised to come right away.

Night had fallen by the time I received a call from the Office. Mom was there, asking for authorization to check me out. It was painful to move from the lodgings to the Office. The lodging was square and my bed, far from the door, shook when I got into or out of it. The beds were double. Bunk beds. My lodging was the third one on the fourth floor. I moved by holding onto the railings, the banisters, and the columns, asking for help from some fellow patient, breathing deeply. The director wanted to check the veracity of my story. He lifted my skirt and observed. Below was my body, naked and broken. The deputy director and the guard observed. Mom too. The four of them understood, covered their noses. The director personally signed the release.

Mom drove me home. It had been a long time since I'd seen the rest of my family. They all hugged me and carried me to my room in their arms. Dad's sister, a neonatal specialist, came over not long after to *examine me*. The examination consisted of a profound, lengthy observation. "I don't dare treat her," she said. "You have to take her to the Hospital." Neonatology deals with babies from one to thirty days. After thirty days, another type of specialist examines children, diagnoses them. That night I slept in my own room, on a real mattress, on a real pillow, with real people around me. I dreamed several times. Not that day or any other have I ever managed to remember what I dreamed. Neonatology is the specialty that deals with babies from one to thirty days. After thirty days, another type of specialist examines children, diagnoses them.

In the Hospital's ER they diagnosed me with gonorrhea. A doctor asked me, very nicely, to take off my clothes and get onto a cot. Dad's neonatologist sister, beside me, gave her approval. When my legs were open, neonatologist and doctor exchanged a look. I perceived astonishment in the exchange, consternation, accusation. I closed my eyes. The doctor put on gloves and inserted a finger into me. Nothing in my life, before that, had ever been so painful, so offensive. I screamed, and Dad's sister whispered in my ear, "It's your own fault." I didn't feel guilty of anything. Or only of having missed classes three days in a row. Which actually made me happy, proud.

Gonorrhea, also known as blennorrhea or gonococcal urethritis, is a sexually transmitted infection provoked by bacteria called gonococcus. Transmission occurs during coitus, or during birth if the mother is infected, or through indirect contamination if a woman uses the personal hygiene products of another person who is infected. Gonorrhea is among the most common sexually transmitted diseases in the world. The non-genital places that are also attacked are the rectum, the pharynx, and the conjunctiva of the eyes. The vulva and the vagina in women, normally, are also affected, as they are connected by epithelial cells. In women, the cervix is usually the first site of infection.

The doctor's opinion did not take into consideration the pelvic inflammation or urinary discomfort; the man based his accusation on the redness of my genitals, the vaginal secretion, and something undeniable: a smell of rotten fish that spread throughout the room.

Mom and Dad, susceptible to his verdict, looked at me sadly and asked, in unison, how I could be so careless, why didn't I take precautions, who had infected me, where had the act taken place, what time of day, how many times. The inappropriateness of the questions made me doubt myself. Maybe I was no longer a hygienic person. Maybe I had interacted more affectionately with one of my classmates than with the rest. I didn't even understand what it was all about. I was suspicious, and I didn't believe in friendship. I was immediately admitted into the Hospital's Infectious Disease unit.

The next day, the initial diagnosis had to be confirmed through blood analysis and a couple of vaginal ultrasounds. I refused the ultrasounds. No one else would open my legs, or accuse me any more, or cover their nose at my stench.

They did the analyses that were referred *urgently*, and no great aberrations were detected, just a little of this and another little of that, and the low index of something and the high index of something else. In general, everything more or less as expected. The ultrasounds were indispensable but I would not authorize them. From the Hospital ER came the medical order to bring me to the Operating Room.

Before going into the OR, an African doctor came to see me. He uncovered and observed me. He was a black man who almost reached the ceiling, maybe two meters tall, maybe two meters and change, strong and muscular, young. The white coat shone on his skin, or maybe he shone under the coat. He smelled of trees. He wasn't wearing gloves. He brought his hand close and touched. His immense hand became a petal. The exam a caress.

In the operating room they anesthetized me so they could do all the ultrasounds they wanted, stick inside me all the speculums they wanted, all the gloved fingers, clamps, pincers, cotton, machines. The anesthesiologist was an obese woman who looked at me like I was a freak. My fear made the snot run and the anesthesiologist whispered in my ear, "If your nose keeps running I won't anesthetize you." Then I dried the mucus on the edge of my hospital gown. Mom was outside crying for me, her sick firstborn. Dad was outside crying for Mom, his weepy wife.

At the end of the day, the operation was a failure. Not gonorrhea, or trichomoniasis, or HPV, or herpes, or chlamydia, or candida. I presented only an intense moniliasis caused by dirty water and an allergic reaction to Nystatin, the cream the doctor in the Clinic had spread days before between my labia, around my clitoris, and on the vaginal wall.

Mom wanted to sue the doctor, the Clinic, the director

and deputy directors of the Hospital, Dad's neonatologist sister, and anyone else they put in front of her. The results were given to her while I was still dreaming under the effect of the anesthesia. I dreamed, sang, danced, spoke, screamed, and cried under the effect of that anesthesia. It was a state of illumination that I've managed to reach very few times since, not even by putting drops of homatropine under my tongue, or inserting little triangles of acid into my anal cavity, or smoking an immense yellow flower alone in my rented apartment. Nothing has been as supreme as those milliliters of general anesthesia.

Four days later I left the Hospital. The cold aloe salves and the intravenous antibiotic resulted in the total recovery of my genital organs. It was still uncomfortable to urinate, because of the impression of the wounds that were still in my body's reflexes, in my memory.

That same night Mom took me to the theater. One of the most important theater festivals was happening in the city, and Mom wanted to reward me. The work was called *Electra Garrigó*, and it was a contemporary version of the Greek *Electra*, brought to the stage so many times. Her mother, Clitemnestra Plá, resembled my mother in many respects. The love/hate relationship between them overlapped a lot with our relationship. I realized that the characters, just like the actors, were suffering a kind of collective hysteria, something I have continued to detest as a form of mediocrity and vulgarity.

Nothing was intense in the scene. Nothing was alive there. There was no pain. There was no ideology. The scream wasn't real. The blow wasn't real. It was racket, speculation, tradition. The Stanislavski Method applied coldly and calculatingly. An audience, equally uniform, was enjoying the show from the seats. Welcome to the carnival. I got up and left. I walked up the ramp of the theater aisle noticing the line of faces beside me. Mom got up and left. She walked up the ramp of the theater aisle without looking at the rest of the audience. Looking at a fixed point that was my head on the horizon. Outside the theater a man was selling candy, popcorn. Those who hadn't gotten tickets had stayed there, talking. "You're ungrateful," she said, and she slapped me in the middle of the street. Inside the theater, people started to applaud.

Be happy
wherever
you go,
you told me one day.
That's why
I don't complain
when I go
anywhere
without you.

LEPIDOPTERA

I have maybe a few days or a few weeks of life left. Maybe a few hours. You've told me you'll still be another month. There won't be time to give you the code, or there will. I'll be optimistic. I only remember there are six numbers. I spend the day trying to remember them, my memory isn't what it used to be. You'll have to go through the library, book by book, page by page. In one of them there's a paper with the numbers written on it.

In the advanced stages an acceptable quality of life can still be obtained, in spite of the critical situation and the side effects that plague me.

The current advancements in radiation and chemotherapy are effective weapons in keeping the pain from wiping me out completely. I was exposed to a surgery. Salvage surgery, they call it. Everything very white and metallic. Several doctors. And nurses. And medical technicians. They were friendly and understanding. I was pleased.

I had to make the decision myself. They didn't believe I was alone in the world. "But I'm not alone in the world," I explained. You're with me even though you're not here. They evaluated the characteristics of the disease, and also the side effects that the metastatic localizations were producing. And all in the context of the host, that is, of the patient himself, of me. They felt bad telling me, but I encouraged them. "Let's do this."

Their considerations allowed me to analyze and arrange the most appropriate therapy, with the sole objective of offering me a better quality of life.

"I have a daughter," I explained to them, "who has just given birth to a nine-pound boy." You haven't told me what you named him, or who he looks like most. Tell me about him.

The most frequent situations in which palliative therapy is needed for a patient have to do with the extent of the neoplastic process and its dissemination toward the different regions or organs that have been invaded. For example: the skeleton, the central nervous system, the liver, the lungs or other cavities, which lead to secondary effusions and bleeding. Which in my case amounts to my whole body. Understand?

They explained to me that the skeleton is one of the most common sites of distant metastasis, specifically produced by malignant neoplasias that originated in the breast, the lung, the prostate, the kidney, or the thyroid. I never thought my prostate would become what it is today. A rotten stone that smells like mud. It's terrible, my dear.

Last night I wrote the exact description of what I was feeling in my notebook. Understand that I have become an old and sensitive man, one who cries when he sees your photograph and who sleeps in your bed with the I.V. in. Can you imagine?

The most important symptoms in the treatment I began are the pain and the neurological disorders resulting from compressions of the spine, which could present at any point along its length. I've already experienced them.

Today at noon, before I swallowed one of those instant soups that I hate so much and are so easy to prepare, your letter came with the photo of the baby. It was the perfect excuse to put off the onion and squash soup and run to the library where I could read it calmly. If only I had run, but it was more like I reached my destination—the library—by dragging myself vertically, my back or side up against the wall, my hands clutching at the columns and the furniture, my feet taking short steps, barely lifting off the floor.

The baby's photo is now in the library, in a new picture frame made to look antique.

They told me I had to bear in mind the possibility of fracture from the weakening of the osseous matter brought on by erosion. That really scared me. So I took precautions, gave away a lot of furniture, arranged the rest of it along the walls; I tried to maintain good taste. Now the house is the way you always wanted it. Modern and minimalist.

These fractures that they warned me of are referred to as spontaneous, because they frequently occur from a simple movement, and they're easily produced in the most deteriorated part of the bone. They are frequent, above all, in people like me, of advanced age, and of course they must be mended through orthopedic surgery. I've been forewarned, don't worry, I move very slowly, like a snail. The kind you liked to collect. Land snails. Polymitas.

Lung cancer, they said, and kidney cancer, and malignant melanoma produce their metastasis in the central nervous system, nearly always. This manifestation can be due to a metastasis in the osseous cranial vault, which then invades the nervous tissue, or the encephalic mass directly. The symptoms that appear most frequently in this localization are cephalea, mental disorders, and problems with motor skills, such as ataxia and aphasia. When I heard that, I laughed. They sound like the names of twin girls who go to the park hand in hand. One wants to play on the swings and the other prefers the merry-go-round. In the end, they decide to get on the teeter-totter, and then they go down the slide. Their mother loses sight of them and calls to them to make sure they're still together. "Ataxia and Aphasia! Where are you?"

Before prescribing a treatment, the doctors carry out the necessary exams to confirm the presence of a cerebral metastasis, and then decide on the most appropriate measure for improving the clinical profile.

At first I didn't understand, but I gradually came to understand. You, too, will understand.

It was important, as well, after the metastasis was diagnosed, to determine whether it was single or multiple. Modern diagnostic methods, such as cerebral scintigraphy, computerized axial tomography, and nuclear magnetic resonance, allowed the diagnosis to be confirmed with enough accuracy.

Today, very early, I opened a book of poems by José Kozer, the last he produced: *Expanding Particles*. Kozer, whom I met once in a New York cafe, made me feel miserable. Not because of the poem I read—*one verdict acts on another verdict, cancels the obsession of its words*—but because I confused those lines to the point that I saw them double and couldn't distinguish the verdict. What would José Kozer say if he saw me, unable to follow his obsession with my eyes. The conversation we had in that cafe is one of my most treasured memories.

*   *   *

Your birth, dear daughter, is also one of my most treasured memories. You were born at seven months. You wanted out as soon as possible.

I met so many people in that cafe. One of them was your mother. She didn't even look at me. She came and went behind the counter, like the doctors in the hospital hallway. Though she moved effectively and no customer ever came to feel badly served, her movements were docile, slippery. I loved the way she set down the mug, perpendicular to me in front of my chest. I came back the next day and ordered something different, so she wouldn't notice. I wanted to see her anonymously, without her knowing she was being seen. Her manner was the same. Docile and slippery.

If it had been a single metastasis, the treatment could have been radiation or the exeresis of the single mass. Chemotherapy, because it is difficult for cytotoxic drugs to pass through the blood-brain barrier, is of little use. What is in fact necessary, I would say obligatory, is to act on the edema through corticosteroids, and to use diuretics to decrease the amount of interstitial liquid, which in turn causes edema.

I'm practically a professional in the matter. We could open our own clinic, if it weren't for the time.

You've told me he was born healthy, the little one. That he opened his eyes right away and stared at you. Marvelous. When you were born you didn't open your eyes until morning. You looked like a bean, a pink and hairy bean.

Your mother, of course, knew José Kozer, and she adored him, like I did. I watched her devour his sentences, learn fragments of his poems, stare at him fixedly in the cafe. Thanks to José Kozer I felt jealousy, that stingy and attractive feeling, impossible like few others to hide. Before she died, your mother gave me a letter for José Kozer that I never mailed him. Like the code, it must be between the pages of some book. If you find it, send it to him yourself. Fulfill her wish. She'll be at peace. We'll both be at peace. The memory will even wrap José Kozer in peace, the happiness of a memory he has surely forgotten.

He'd come in, sit down, order a green tea, take out a sheet of paper and a pen. He didn't write anything until half an hour later, once he'd seen and heard a few incoherent phrases coming and going around him.

One day I waited for him to come in, sit down, order his tea, take out his paper and pen, all in order. Then I went over, sat down across from José Kozer, ordered a cappuccino, sipped it slowly, and told him: "I'm going to burn your books, so she can't read them." The man said to me: "Don't burn them, sell them."

Compression of the spinal cord is one of the most high-pressure emergencies in oncology. I saw the doctors come and go down those hallways, crazed over a spine. There can be progressive and irreversible damage if they're slow to diagnose and, as a result, slow to administer appropriate treatment. Although to be honest, my dear, it's all irreversible at this point. The distance between you and me, for example, is the same as a compression.

And so, the treatment of that type of lesion will consist of surgical decompression through the resection of the tumor, though partial, followed by radiation of the damaged area. The secondary complications that arise are unconnected to the direct influence of the neoplasia. What happens is that, needing repose and bed rest for a prolonged period of time with limited movement, bedsores and ulcers are inevitably produced. So, adequate hygiene is necessary, and treatment with stimulants for endothelial activation. The wounds improve and even scar over.

However, my dear, the pain continues. The anxiety, the fear, and the desperation are accompanied by an unbearable pain that leads to depression. The desire to see you again keeps me standing. The doctors, sometimes, see me smile, and they're surprised by the shine in my eyes. That's you in my eyes. And it's him in my eyes. If I saw him and didn't have the muscular strength to hold him in my arms, I'd know all this effort wasn't worth it.

Right now, as I type the word *now*, the pain takes over my abdominal area and is devastating; I vomit onto my feet, the nurse will clean it up. I'll drag myself to bed, lie down a while. I'll try again to remember the code, and if not, you'll find it stuck between two random pages of a magnificent book.

My tumor is like me, a mollusk. It carries its house on its back. I am its house. It has slid determinedly inside me, through me, with me. Its triumph is nigh. We both know it.

Alternating contractions and elongations of its organism, slow and devastating, it got the upper hand and made room.

The snail grows and so does its shell.

Every one of its logarithmic spirals penetrates a little further, ever deeper.

I must have housed at least two of them, so they could couple and reproduce. Female/male one, and female/male another, they reproduced. Their eggs, scattered everywhere, populated the place.

The snail is large and bitter.

The snail's life, between five and seven years, overtook my life.

Like in books, the hero and anti-hero were intertwined. Nothing closer to that love-hate relationship that paramours enjoy.

When the snail dies, its house dies too.

José Kozer's poems about what he considers a house are delicious treats.

I'm sorry for talking to you so much about poetry.

The library is large and the books are your greatest inheritance, shake them and care for them, and above all, open them. If they seem very thick, tedious, impenetrable, pause on a word that you find at random. Investigate its meaning for yourself. Each book is much more than words on paper. I, for example, love typographies, illustrations, the titles of poems, or of chapters. There tends to be a whole life science in the brief sentences, another kind of love, which also hurts.

It's all yours.

It belongs to you only.

Feelings
and hemorrhoids:
when they start
to emerge externally,
the most advisable thing
is bed rest.

SINAI

BLIND

At dawn I reached Mount Sinai, where I knew sacrifice to be common and everyday. I looked over my shoulder at the path I had followed to get there and I found it hostile, rocky. I knelt down and began to talk with God, to tell him what had happened to me so far and to tell him that I still remained fearful of him, because God was the greatest I had ever known. Salvation. A raft in the ocean.

The conversation began to lengthen and turn into requests I made of God without the slightest respect or shame. God help me with this and God help me with that. God I need this and I need that. God protect these and God protect those, who are my family and friends, and even protect my enemies who deep down are good people. God take my brother out of my life. Take him far away from me, that man who is no longer the man I've known since I was born. Take him as far away as your magnificence is able. I don't want to carry that weight. I don't want to meet him in my own house. I don't want his legal address to be my own house. Before you oh God who knows me and knows that I am your servant and that I have struggled so to be good, a servant of God. Oh great highest Lord, grant me that, and I will not ask you for anything else.

Then you looked down on me from on high, my God, and you took my sight. I never saw anything again. Not my brother or my husband or my mother. I've never again seen the food I eat, or the clothes I wear, or the fingernails the manicurist paints for me at her beauty parlor. I've never again seen the floral arrangements in the Church, oh God. I've never turned my eyes upward again. Alleluia.

DEAF

At dawn I reached Mount Sinai, where I knew God's majesty was everywhere, that its strength and faith was dispersed all around and constituted the place. I turned my head around in an empty gesture of sensing the path I had followed to get there, and I found it hostile, dark.

The bit about darkness was just feminine intuition. I knelt down on a rock and closed my eyelids because that's how a servant of God speaks with her Father, Jesus's Father and mine, oh God, how I love you. I thanked him for letting me arrive safe and sound, I gave thanks for the food that had already run out, and for the food that he would surely provide me with in the coming hours. I gave thanks for my life and for the things in life that he offered me and that he offers daily to all his children, no distinction or preferences. I told him everything that had happened to me so far. The tribulations a sinner woman like me goes through every day, walking down a road stalked by scroungers, beggars, and people— that is, strangers.

More and more I needed to get to the point, so I spoke to God of the matter that had brought me there.

It's my brother my God, I can't stand it anymore, his voice pounding in my ears morning, noon, and night. It's my brother my God again in the city, again in my house, again in my life. Take him from my life my God I don't deserve this. You know Father that I bow before you in fear but the truth is I just can't bear him. Have mercy on this servant of yours and take him far away where I cannot hear him.

And then oh God you made your presence great and large toward me, and you struck me deaf. I never again heard my brother's voice or anyone else's. My mother's voice and that of my husband are movements of the mouth I do not recognize. I've never again heard music or the horrendous noises of the carnivals. No sound for me oh master of all creatures.

MUTE

I reached Mount Sinai. Dawn was breaking. My eyelids were heavy as a couple of buckets of water. Everything felt heavy and it still feels heavy today oh Father how I praise you. Alleluia Father I no longer know from whence I came. I've forgotten where I came from, what my nationality is, where I live. The dead roots I've seen and left behind, the shrubs, the thorns, and the mushrooms, mean only time. Time is yours my God, and I know I am the most blessed woman right now, for I shall now prostrate myself before you Lord.

I do not hear you, do not see you, but I can still speak in my tongue, and you do see me, and you do hear me, the way you see and hear your servants, who in your name have been born and who your name serve.

My brother has returned home, Lord. Our mother opened the door and there was my brother, and I am sure his rough arms were crossed over his chest and that smile I hate was spreading across his face. Do your will my God, and free us of his presence, of his smell, of his voice, and his gaze. He is of the world Father, he does not serve you. He says he believes in you but he does bad and dirty things, and we know it and it repels us, and we feel such repulsion for him.

Then oh God I felt your light and your breath, and your divine warmth, and I lacked my tongue to continue speaking. In its place a hollow space, and further back my throat, with its astonished tonsils, and further back my esophagus, surprised, and so on.

I still wonder what I said wrong, Lord.

I'm still lost and it seems dawn is breaking.

It seems that any moment I'll intuit the first highway, the first bus, a house.

What you like
most about me
is that I'm
like you.
Tomorrow
morning
I'm going to change
my name.

TATTOO

A man sees another man with tattoos and he asks himself if
   that man was in prison.
People ask themselves questions they can answer them-
   selves, and the answer combines with their beliefs.
I ask myself if a man who sees my tattoos wonders if I was
   in prison.
And the answer combines with my beliefs.
But I'm wrong, that's not the answer.
The truth is that yes, I was in prison.
Every time I went to prison I got a tattoo.

In the women's prison, one woman gives another a tattoo,
and that woman asks her to do it with care.
So they're tattoos born of love.
It hurts because it burns.
The tattoo.
And the love.

The women who give tattoos in prison are almost always
butch. Out of sixteen women who've given me tattoos
in prison, eleven have been butch, one more or less, and
four not at all.
Right away they want to protect me and keep me and marry
me. I ask myself how we're going to get married and
the reply is an *impossible* that bleeds like a tattoo. We're
never going to get married.
I don't care about getting married or not. What's important
to me is to maintain my beliefs, and to get ever-prettier
tattoos.
In jail there are no colors.
That's what I steal.
Colors.
Needles.

Machines.

I steal them from professional tattoo studios, which in reality aren't professional at all.

Just shit, is what they are.

Come on.

The only one responsible for my problems is me.

I'm drastic that way.

My mom taught me that.

That where the mule drops is where he gets the whip.

And I've been lucky with lawyers, who've always defended
me tooth and nail.

Lawyers are another story.

No lawyer has ever wanted to marry me.

But I'm cool.

All in all.

None of them know how to give tattoos.

The last lawyer took me to see a movie one weekend and
in the middle of the movie he put his arm around my
shoulders and pinched my nipple.

Right away I knew what he wanted.

I touched it and the poor guy was about to explode.

He lasted a minute.

I won't tell you his name because it would be unethical.

I was left wanting to see more movies.

Once I wore a doctor's coat into a hospital to see if I could
get gloves.

Because a guy was going to give me a free tattoo if
I brought him a box of gloves with a hundred pairs,
minimum.

The tattoo was going to be crazy.

Enormous.

Coming up like this along my arm, onto my shoulder, and
finishing over my clavicle.

What it was going to be I didn't know, but the guy had
a ton of magazines and he drew beautifully.

When a guy draws like that you say he's got the touch.

So that's what this guy had.

The touch.

The day we agreed on our deal he gave me the touch until
I came.

He sat me on his legs, lifted my shirt and got started.

Some people just like to do the work themselves.

Instead of telling me to take off my clothes.

Then he said I should marry him, that he likes animals like
I do, and that he was going to cover me with beautiful
tattoos.

I miss my family so much that the last tattoo I got was in
their honor.

NO LOVE LIKE A MOTHER'S LOVE.

That's what I got.

Because in the end, when it comes to the family, the mother
is the main thing.

Along my whole left arm.

Letters in cursive.

Is that how you say it?

And check this out, it was the word *mother* that got infected.

I almost got lymphangitis.

But thank God, it scarred over well.

In any case, one day I'm going to touch it up, even if it's
just the word *mother*.

When it comes to tattoos, you've got to rise to the occasion.

You can't drink rum, or even beer, after getting a tattoo.

You can't do you-know-what, either.

Yes, that.

For a brand-new tattoo, soap and water is the best thing.

If it's really necessary, Gentamicin or any other antibiotic.

I apply Heparin if I can get a prescription, because
the pharmacies won't sell you anything without
a prescription.

I have a friend at a pharmacy who was in jail with me.

She hooks me up sometimes, but not always.

And I don't push it because otherwise, she's looking for
trouble.

And she's a coward.

Not like me.

I'm pretty sure that woman doesn't have a single tattoo.

My only enemy is me.

Sometimes I go crazy.

I freak out.

Tattoos are a drug.

Once you get the first one you want the second and the
third.

And it's never-ending.

And they have to be odd.

For example, you can't have eight, or ten, it always has to
be an odd number.

My favorites are the ones you see, but I have a lot you don't
see unless I'm naked.

And I'm not going to get naked now.

I'm too embarrassed with you.

And with all of them.

How many?

Twenty-nine so far.

I got the first one in middle school.

My middle school, Ana Betancourt, had really strange
architecture.

One afternoon I played hooky and got the tattoo.

Twelve years old exactly.

I fell in love with a guy who looked like my grandfather.

The guy gave me rum and bought me a gold chain.

And a ring too.

Fool's gold.

I remember as if it happened today the way my dad bawled
at me when I got home.

"You don't know how many cells you killed," he bawled.

Over a million.

My dad is the most intelligent guy I've ever met, along with

the lawyers.
But I don't regret it.
It was a heart, my first tattoo.

Not to brag, but my tattoos are really something to see.
On a farm where they put me to work once, those women
    just went crazy.
Really.
One woman comes up on me and she says, "I want to give
    you a tattoo on your ass," and I tell her, "Do it."
We get everything ready and the woman starts.
Turns out what she wanted was to see my ass.
Check this out, she cleaned off the ink with her tongue.
And I was happy as can be because with the tongue it burns
    less.
She tattooed a sunflower on my ass.
An incomplete sunflower because there was no yellow ink,
    so the woman could only tattoo the outline.
Afterward I saw it in a mirror.
Truly beautiful.
The center of the sunflower is my ass, all covered in little
    dots, the way sunflowers are.

When I got pregnant my mother came right away.

She brought a letter from my dad.

My dad, so smart, only said in his letter that the most
    important thing in life was to know who you are.

How's that for a laugh?

At that moment and with that message.

Know who you are, how about that.

My mom wanted to know who the baby's father was.

If only it were a lawyer.

But it wasn't a lawyer.

It was a Rastafarian who did American-style tattoos.

That's what he said, but I didn't know what he meant by
    American-style.

He gave me a tattoo of a skull, and not just any skull, an
    original one, with a leg shaped like a parasol.

What a laugh.

That Rastafarian never even found out I got pregnant.

With a skull and a baby.

My mom wanted to know what I planned to name it.

"After you, if it's a girl."

After he was born, my mom took him with her.

I didn't want her to take him but she was afraid I'd give him
    a tattoo. I'd have to be crazy to do that.

They went to live in the countryside, my mom, my dad,
    and my son.

The countryside far from the city.

My dad sent me a letter telling me that the boy likes
    animals, same as me. And I was very happy because ani-
    mals keep you company when you're alone. They give
    you love. They get sad if you don't love them. They
    learn everything you tell them.

They never betray you. They swallow everything without
    complaint.

Even if it's nothing but rice.

Today the boy must be three years old.

My mom hasn't even told me what his name is.

Fear of death is ridiculous.

Now that I know everything and I have to take so many
    pills, I'm at my calmest.

The doctors told me nice and clear that in my situation,
    even a cold will kill me.

Here it's also like a prison.

Worse, because there are no women who ask me to marry
    them.

There's no fun.

It was when I got the warrior woman tattoo.

Seven colors: black, dark blue, light blue, violet, red,
orange, and yellow.

It's a rainbow, a spotlight.

Only to be seen by one who loves me.

Seems the guy didn't change the needle.

Or the gloves.

Or the machine had sick blood.

Or whatever.

These things happen and we can't be afraid.

It didn't even cross my mind that you can get sick that way.

The tattoo turned out right on.

It didn't even get infected.

The good thing is I won't have to keep going from place
to place.

No family.

No house.

A body without family isn't a person.

Aren't you going to ask me what Cuba means to me?

Look.

The map of Cuba, I got it tattooed in ninety-nine.

As a young girl.

By the same guy I told you about, with the gloves.

Who's rough but I like it.

And none of that outline shit.

No.

Filled in.

On the ribs, where it hurts the most.

Man, your nation is your nation.

We were
at a bar
and we had
to leave.
It was the guy
who brought
the cocktails—
not only was
he a man,
he was really rude.

TREE

I live alone and still. I sleep a lot, for hours. I'm correcting a study I wrote last year so I could graduate. I'm correcting it so I can send it in to a contest that an android told me about. The prize is three thousand dollars. I need money so I can move. I want to live in front of the ocean. In a clean and empty apartment. It's empty where I live, but not clean. Filth surrounds me at a conceptual level of the word. It surrounds and absorbs me. I am part of it, although I know that's temporary. If I manage to win the prize I will no longer be part of the filth. If I don't win I'll do something else. I've outlined a plan to go and work. I've been an actress, but I don't want to do that anymore. I'm interested in anthropology. And sleeping. I sleep for up to twelve hours a day, then I get up and smile. I have large teeth, and when I smile I spread harmony all around.

I walk everywhere. With headphones on and music in my brain. When I walk along a street or turn a corner, I don't see misery or hear the men tell me, "Mami, I'd fuck you so good, I'd lick it till you died." My brain functions to the beat of the music. The social system around me, politics and the economy, are songs I dance to along a path of mud, mangy animals, old food. There's so much aggressiveness in the world.

The android who told me about the prize promises to help me correct my text. In the first paragraph, for example, there are three instances in a row of "so I could/can," which constitutes a grammatical mistake. If I want to enter and win, I have to clean up the writing so it can be read like a pool of water. Clear and fluid. The android is a writer. He has published small books at small publishing houses. We've known each other for years. We live in the same city and now we live very close to each other. He's acquired some new buttons and he looks better, younger, happier. I'm still the same. Younger and happier.

*　*　*

The subject of my research is a theater group called the Enchanted Deer. I've been part of this group for four years and I know its inner workings. During those four years I've investigated and written. Title of the study: "El muerto se fue de rumba: The Notion of Being in the Enchanted Deer." I've divided the work into two chapters. The first chapter includes the theoretical-practical foundations for the creation of Being in the Enchanted Deer, and the second chapter analyzes the Beings. The idea of Being is not an invention of the Enchanted Deer. It's someone else's invention. "Who invented it?" the android whispers beside me at the bar.

My research consists not of the answer, but of a continuous enigma of creativity. The high ritualistic content of each performance by the Enchanted Deer awakened my interest, inspired a curiosity and attraction that were explosive, essential. I decided to take aptitude tests to join the group as an actress. And I made it. I joined the group. The journey began.

I see altars dedicated to some intellectual, spiritual deities, which I won't find in other temples or down other religious holes. I see offerings made to spirits who watch us every day, ashamed. I touch the offerings and I'm transformed. "Look and don't touch," murmur the members of the Enchanted Deer, winding three circles around my neck.

On Sunday we go to a bar with a friend who came in from Madrid. The name of the bar pays homage to one of the least accomplished films by Fernando Pérez. His cinematographic work includes films like *Clandestinos*, *Madagascar*, *La vida es silbar*, and *Suite Habana*. True works of art, monstrous and universal. The rest is dry leaves, still lifes. To get to the bar we walked for a kilometer, the android, my friend, and I. The streets from east to west are named with letters of the alphabet and from north to south with numbers. It's one of the prettiest neighborhoods in the country. But it's not my favorite. The place I want to move to is at the end of a tunnel. There is coast and open sea.

The ocean, in my brain, no longer has its own definition. It's not a mass of salty water but rather a song that exists, day and night, in spite of the violence and the beauty. Seas are differentiated mainly by their contact with the ocean, and can be open or closed. If a sea is surrounded almost entirely by land then we speak of an inland sea, while if it's very open we speak of a marginal sea.

I had a sailor father who turned into a tree. I go visit him and the tree doesn't even move its branches. Genetically, some day I will also turn into a tree. It's in my blood. Every time he came back from his secret missions, he went to bed with this woman, my mother, and got her pregnant. That's how my siblings and I were born. It would seem that getting my mother pregnant was ultimately his most important mission, the end point. But no, turning into a tree was the end point. Every one of my brothers and sisters and I have our own watering cans. I tell this story about my father to the android while we're on the way to the bar. When we've nearly reached the bar the android asks me, "What did your mother become?"

The notion of Being is closely related to Jerzy Grotowski's theory of the performer, in which he explains that a performer is not one who pretends to be another, not one who acts out characters, but rather one who develops a *channel organism* through which forces circulate, while he remains himself in front of others, showing himself, acting as a bridge between memory and pure forms. "I don't ever want to live under a bridge," whispers the android beside me at the bar. "Me neither," I tell him, staring straight at him.

To enact this theory, Jerzy Grotowski developed a technique that he called the "negative path," which tries to eliminate physical and psychic blockages impeding expression, in order to enter that creative state, to touch intimate and unknown places within the actor and expose them to the public. It's a job that, instead of creating skills, eliminates them in order to delve deeper into the unknown. In the book *Towards a Poor Theater*, Jerzy Grotowski states that the "negative path" is a process of elimination. The actor must discover the resistances and obstacles that keep him from achieving a creative task. The exercises are a way to overcome personal impediments. The actor must not ask himself, *How should I do this?* but rather must know what he should not do, what stands in his way. He has to personally adapt to the exercises to find a solution that eliminates the obstacles, which are different in each actor. "Are you in love with Jerzy Grotowski?" whispers the android beside me at the bar. "Not me, are you?" I whisper to him. Then we start to kiss.

We leave the bar drunk, the android, my friend, and I. Our walk recalls characters by Severo Sarduy or Reinaldo Arenas, our arms around one another while we're falling down laughing, me and the android kissing behind the trees along the sidewalk. The android has an iPod with an amplifier. He carries it in his hand like a music box. "It *is* a music box," he tells me. "You are music and I am music." At every tree we kiss behind the android asks me, "Does your father look like this tree?"

Really, the trees in this city annoy me. So pruned and clipped they seem artificial. They seem rootless and un-perennial. In my brain I've drawn up a list of famous trees: baobab, eucalyptus, willow, birch, pine, fir, ceiba, chestnut, maple, cedar, cypress. "I would like to kiss you behind a cypress," the android whispers to me like a lecherous child. I think about how this tree, where we are now, has the same genetic information as my heart.

They kicked us out of the bar. We don't need that bar to have fun. A bar that pays homage to Fernando Pérez's worst movie. They should be ashamed. They should come and apologize to us. The bar's owner found us in the bathroom, kissing, with the iPod and speaker turned all the way up, and the bar's owner didn't find it charming, he found it obscene, a disgrace. He made a motion like he was going to hit us; my friend came in, shoved him; he shoved us.

* * *

The year two thousand and one marks the beginning of a very personal exploration by each of the Enchanted Deer's members on the subject of illness, and the central text of that investigation was the novel *Beach Birds*, by Severo Sarduy. Severo Sarduy has been considered one of our members since nineteen ninety-eight. The discovery of his work contributed to defining the poetics of the Enchanted Deer, based on the connection between the narrative language put forth by Severo Sarduy and theatrical language. In terms of the relationship between Severo Sarduy's work and that of the Enchanted Deer, I would point to how neither are informational in nature, but rather are metaphorical; their interest is not in telling a story, but in showing a situation that puts the reader/spectator into a certain physical state. This is one of the reasons why working with sensation is the basis of the Enchanted Deer. "I am sick," whispers the android behind one of the trees, "and I'm going to turn into an enchanted deer, or a golden antelope, I'm not sure."

Another particularity that brings the works of Severo Sarduy and the Enchanted Deer closer is the relationship between body and writing, which the author himself engaged with through his creative process. He considered writing to be a physical exercise, and he would do a dance for finding the precise word until the word appeared. His work's intention lay in provoking pleasure that was not intellectual but rather sensory, its impulse to invade the reader, absorb him. "So my writing is my sexuality?" the android asks me, his red button lit up.

The decision to sleep at his house is made by all three of us. His house, located at a mid-point between where we are standing and my house, seems like a real paradise at this hour. We go up four flights of stairs, down a hallway, and inside. The apartment is narrow and short. When I look to see what's licking my legs, I find a purebred French bulldog, black and white with a square head. All three of us flop down in an enormous bed between flowered sheets that don't match anything. The android and I keep kissing a while longer, playful and regretful, we've known each other by sight for so long now. The French bulldog careens from the bathroom and plops between us like a soccer ball. The android lifts him up like a dead weight by the tough skin of his back, puts him in the living room, orders him to sleep. But at that hour the bulldog no longer wants to sleep. He wants to give love.

The android calls me two or three times a day. Every time he reads a page of my study, he calls me. He sounds distant and I don't know him. He makes me laugh with funny anecdotes, but I don't know him. There's such stillness here. He's converted the PDF into a Word document and given new names to my chapters. He's added italics and erased the acknowledgments. He's broken up the chapters, added and subtracted pages. He's said that some accent marks are missing, but it's not my fault, it was the laptop keyboard's fault. He's changed the first person plural to the first person singular. "It's not a thesis anymore," whispers the android over the phone. "It's got to be a book." "Don't call me anymore," I whisper to him, and I hang up the phone.

I live alone and still. Sometimes it hurts and sometimes it doesn't. In the Enchanted Deer, pain is a path toward knowledge. To constantly overcome one's limits is what brings the body to another state of consciousness, where it can rediscover the real functioning of our organism, making the body into a technique.

The goal, as in all moments of training, is to connect the things that we've grown accustomed to dispersing. In this case, to achieve this unified state, one passes through the pain threshold. This reminds me of the words of Marina Abramovi , a performance artist who also works in this key and posits in her documentary *The Artist is Present*, centered on an exhibit at the Museum of Modern Art: "*Yes, pain exists. But the pain is like a secret. The moment you cross the pain threshold, you enter into another mental state. There is a feeling of beauty and of unconditional love, that feeling that there are no walls between your body and the medium that surrounds you. Then you start to feel incredibly light, in harmony with yourself.*"

My buttocks are also large, round, and taut, and they harmonize with the rest of the house. A pine stairway leads to a second, handcrafted room, where I sleep for hours on a mattress on the wood floor. There is dust everywhere, and also darkness. In the darkness the dust is invisible. I want to move.

Even though I told him not to, the android called and he says he's coming over. I decide to receive him in my dark, homespun room; we could dance, he always has his music box. He arrives at nine thirty. He has the music box and an external hard drive full of movies and documentaries. The laptop doesn't have much space left but I'll copy up to the last gig of capacity. I ask him to please make recommendations. The android recommends, nervous. I copy several directors. I copy Yorgos Lanthimos, Leos Carax, Todd Solondz, François Ozon, and Michael Haneke. I copy videos on art, literature, and jazz.

The android is absorbed in the green line of the program for copying and pasting files. I take his fingers softly. I look at him. He has piercings in and around his face. One in the left eyebrow, another in the right ear, another in the cartilage of his nose. "And another in my tongue," he whispers. "Let's see," I tell him. "Stick out your tongue." When he sticks it out I bring my lips close and bite the tip, pain. "And another two in my nipples, I'll show you if you put on music," whispers the android beside me on the mattress. And of course, I put it on.

Exercise brings you to a mental state where anxieties and insecurities disappear. It leaves the exerciser in a higher state of concentration and eliminates most of the parasitical thoughts that are always circling. This is a vital step in accessing the other, where the goal is to clear away thoughts and keep the mind blank for as long as possible so the body can flow organically, without reason getting in the way.

The Enchanted Deer doesn't work with calisthenics because they tend to disconnect mind, body, and spirit. Calisthenics are also known as *warm-ups*. They're a set of exercises that use only muscular movements with the purpose of developing physical strength.

I had a laborer mother who developed her physical strength and then turned into an appliance. When someone plugs her in, she unplugs herself on her own. It's very uncomfortable because you have to be always coming and going to plug her in. I, for example, cannot *unplug*. Taxes have gone up since this woman became what she became. My siblings and I have drawn up a plan to pay the electricity between us all, even though none of us live in that house anymore. It seems that making us spend money has been our mother's end point. I consider end points to always be unpleasant. Outside, the tree is motionless.

The android
I most loved
had no sex,
no heart,
and no TV.
Nothing
to offer me.

BAD

The thing is that I'm sitting on the curb of a more or less large airport. Not as big as the ones in Madrid or Berlin, but yes, pretty big. I've been here for thirty-six hours and no one has come to check my ticket, or ask me what I'm doing here, or kick me out of here, so I say to myself, *This is what you wanted?* Naturally, I did not want this. What I wanted was to get back all the time lost over the past six months and up to this very minute.

I've ordered an Americano with cream, our favorite, to warm me up. The mug in my hands acts as a heater for my body. The heat from the ceramic penetrates and does me good, so much good. Then the first sip, and the second, and the third work the same way inside me. They warm me, dry that part that is so sodden.

I'm wearing a Gap dress, blue—*from Miami*—and some round black sunglasses—*from Puerto Rico*—that are in style in all the countries. Sitting on the curb holding the steaming coffee, I constitute a static and instalational ensemble. Why do people see distress when they look into my sunglasses? Why did the chess pieces run out of strategies? And worse, why did they emigrate from the board to my blank page? Wait, what am I talking about.

I came to find you but you weren't here. I looked everywhere. In the houses, the basements and attics, in the parks and squares, in the supermarkets, in the hospitals, in the theaters, in the bookstores, in the multiplexes, in the red light district, in the marihuana plantations, in the desert, in the morgue. I only missed this airport because when I arrived I went running out to look for you without thinking you might still be here. And here you still are. And you don't recognize me.

I was invited to a world poetry festival and I accepted. And I came on an airline that I'd never flown before. The festival reserved my ticket and I was in like Flynn, the festival paid me a stipend, and I went out to find you. It was more than two hundred and fifty dollars, all invested in looking for you until I found you. Though I did have to give talks in hostile places, like a poor, black community on a riverbank that you can only reach by air or water.

I looked for you among the black people, poor and barefoot. I took a boat on the river, I peered into the houses, asked policemen if they hadn't seen you. I couldn't explain the masks. No one was going to believe that someone was traipsing around in a mask without calling attention to herself.

The thing about the masks is inexplicable. No one would understand if I said that a mood is a mask, a political position is a mask, a logical reaction is a mask, an attitude toward life is a mask. The masks accumulate, one on top of the other, so that a person is never, ever exposed. It's funny.

But no one would understand, especially not at a World Poetry Festival, which fights for World Peace and hoists aloft, like a flag, a phrase that's pretty uncomfortable to say. The phrase is stamped on posters all over the city, it's stamped on the complimentary sweatshirt they gave me and on the sweatshirt of each participant, stamped over the entrance to the hotel and on our foreheads when we read poems in a plaza or a camp for displaced persons. Repeat with me: *Peace for all, world spring*.

The thing is that I haven't changed much. Maybe I'm skinnier and more malnourished, scrawnier and sadder from these six months of searching, but my face is still the same, even the piercing and the tattoo are still there. You're the one who has changed, but I recognize you. I'd recognize you even if you yanked out your eyes and were covered in ticks. All these nights I've dreamed of ticks, those fat little bugs that suck the blood of puppies. I've dreamed that they fall from the sky and cover me and suck my blood.

I would rather be covered in ticks than write a book of poems about which the specialized critics say: *precise and correct*. Moreover, I would rather be covered in ticks than never see you again, laughing there in front of me. I don't care if that smiling face of yours is a mask, or if that other face you have now is another mask, or if that other face you wear when you don't agree with something is another mask. I don't care about your masks, infinite and lovely. I don't care about all those characters. Because deep down there's a person, who is you, and I have come to find you.

I would also rather go around dirty, covered in piss and shit, than write a book of poems about which the specialized critics say: *happy and effective*. Moreover, I would rather go an entire year without bathing than write any of those books the specialized critics pay lip service to by spouting bullshit. And I would rather accept any opinion from the specialized critics, including bullshit, including bullshit about tradition and generation, than never see you again, raging before me.

The festival featured readings by men and women from all over the world. The organizers treated us with such kindness that at times I wondered whether they were wearing masks or not. They must have been wearing them, of course.

One day they called my room to invite me to the *airport*, which is a local expression that means to smoke, to get high. So I set off for the *airport* along with the organizers, and I smoked and got high, like a little airplane or bird or a little train among the clouds of a tolerance zone.

I looked for you in that zone and I thought I saw you. You were a little airplane or bird or a little train among the clouds, like me. I went over to the person I thought was you and that person gave me a kiss on the nose and hugged me. You would have kissed my nose and you would have hugged me, but you would never have whispered in my ear what that person whispered to me. A poem by Mario Benedetti. I turned and ran.

Because of that I was paranoid for the rest of the week, looking over my shoulder in case someone came to whisper Mario Benedetti poems into my ear. It didn't matter which ear, the problem was Benedetti.

Another day they invited me again to fly in that zone and I didn't want to, I thanked them and stayed static in the room, and I didn't dare go down to the restaurant for lunch, afraid of running into the organizers on the stairs or in the hall or in the restaurant itself.

The thing is that I knew that's how you were, and that what I was seeing for the first time before me wasn't a person but a mask. But I also knew that beneath the mask was the person and I liked the idea a lot. A person's got to be very brave to use a mask, to even use several masks a day. The risks you run grow ever more dangerous. Like the risk of not knowing who you really are.

I know who I really am because I don't have masks to confuse me. I'm not brave enough to use them, but I've been brave enough to face customs, planes, layovers, the mess of luggage, the scanners, dogs, and ticks. I've faced it all and I've come to look for you. For the person who deep down you are.

I know who I really am and I'm prepared to accept it, even in writing.

I'm the one who does everything around the house, sweep, cook, make the bed, wash the dog, buy the food, and who later complains about doing everything, though it's always done with love.

I'm the one who eats on the sly, straight from the pressure cooker, with all the lights off in the house and the refrigerator door open, at three fifty-seven in the morning.

I'm the one who breaks up with her current partner and starts a relationship with the woman who was with her no-longer-current partner five years ago.

I'm the one who gets bored of relationships approximately one year and six months in.

I'm the one who takes the dog to boring and tedious poetry readings so the poets will be entertained and will look at me with those little faces of bicentennial intellectuals.

I'm the one who's writing this story at dawn, at exactly six-oh-seven, shameless, because they're going to pay me five dollars if I send it to an online photography magazine.

I'm the one who hugs the pillow when I sleep, if you're not there.

I'm the one who doesn't know how to wash by hand, not underwear, not regular clothes, not bedding.

I'm the one who gets a tattoo at random before I figure out what it really means to me.

I'm the one who can't write with someone sleeping in my bed.

I'm the one who gets tired of writing and goes back to join you in bed.

I'm the one who comes in the blink of an eye if you touch that part for a second.

Sometimes I tell lies.

I can delight in a lie for a while, but I don't have masks.

The person I really enjoyed meeting at this world poetry festival was a bald, bearded guy named Pietro Aretino. They scheduled this guy during the same blocks of readings as me and we went around together like husband and wife. His poems and mine were a good pairing, the audiences had fun, and he and I entertained each other. Our meeting was indeed a success. And the spring was between his legs, and between my legs too.

Pietro Aretino is Italian, he makes poems and he makes theater, and not only that but he doesn't use masks. A true weirdo. We should have gotten married and been husband and wife, for real. And had twelve sons and named them after the twelve apostles, or else eleven sons and named them after the players of our favorite soccer team, or our least favorite. We were the happiest couple at the festival. Both a little stressed about the matter of poems read in other languages and the matter of poems not well-received by the audiences, who wanted to know about current politics in our home countries. Pietro Aretino and I behaved as if we weren't from any country. The most tattered and eccentric. And the ones who protested the most.

We didn't want to read in that community that can only be reached by air or by water. With a temperature of forty degrees and a relative humidity of I-don't-know-what percentage. Once in the community, poor Pietro Aretino walked through the muddy streets and turned into a ball of mud. Me too, another little ball of mud. Wet, grumpy, with our poems up our sleeves, unable to read them to anyone who cared about literature. *Peace for all!*

The poems he read beside me are from a book that he will call *Love & Psycho*, a pretty beautiful detail. And the ones I read alongside him are from a book I will call *Give Me Spray*, a detail no less significant.

It's true that if you're not actually a person deep down, my mistake would be fatal. The fear of ridicule pursues us all, and in this case I would be the most ridiculous in history. Coming and going behind a mask that is a mask that is a mask, to the end.

The thing is that in the end I've found you and I've observed you for thirty-six hours. In that time you have used a dozen masks and you've behaved with the customers in very different ways. Only once have you turned around and adjusted your mask. None of the customers caught it, only me, who knows you and knows who you are.

This is happening now.

Again you turn, no mask and a gun in your hand. To my surprise you turn your face toward me. Your face, your gun, and you, the whole package turns toward me. So at the last minute you've recognized me. You like what you see, that's what the mask expresses. You like the dress I chose, blue, with straps. You like the Gap and Desigual and H&M and Zara. You like my round black sunglasses because they're in, and my glasses, specifically, are not cookie cutter, they have

aluminum frames and some initials inside the arms that iden-
tify them, and they're not made in China like all the industrial
products of our time. A halo of elegance mixed with my usual
informality.

You point your gun at me. You walk toward me. You put
the barrel perpendicular to my chest. Several seconds pass and
you decide to raise it perpendicular to my forehead. Several
more seconds pass and you decide to put it between my lips.
My lips give way.

I'm not going to deny the fact that I'm nervous and
delighted, at the same time. Nervous because of the barrel
and delighted because of you, that you've recognized me.
Delighted for the first time in the past six months up to this
very minute.

I know
that I love you.
And that I'm
capable of anything
for you.
But am I really
sure
of that?

SOBA

The initial idea of this book, according to the author—who is not me, I'm just her pet and her instrument of inspiration— was to write fifteen stories, all in the first person so the reader would feel closer to the text. And all of it based on me. About me. So far it's going well, this is the last text, number fifteen, but there's not a trace of me anywhere.

I mean that there's no trace of my real and conclusive and developed presence, the kind that would justify the book's title. I've only made subtle appearances in those interesting phrases she places between one story and the next. And if I'm honest I don't find them that amusing. Clever phrases she comes up with all the time and writes as her Facebook status and then people click *like* on.

Maybe she should have focused more. I saw her writing all the time and not sleeping, she'd sleep maybe three hours at a time, and I wondered what she could be writing. Because she's all for writing two or three books at the same time, she starts a project one day, then comes up with another project and starts that one too, and she doesn't stop until they're both finished, which is exhausting, and something for which a person needs great talent and intelligence, and I don't know if that's really her.

The other day, for example, she got up from her chair and started to make coffee. She looked at me sideways and she said, "Does it really have to come to this, to the point where I scold you, yell at you, throw a flip-flop in your eye?" and all because I went running to the bed, jumped onto the bed, grabbed whatever was closest to the edge of the bed—which was a pair of black leggings and a Forever 21 bra—and I chewed them and shook them and played with them until I turned them into a handful of black shreds. I can't tell if she likes that or not.

The thing about the flip-flop in the eye is just a saying. The way she's found to train me and make me respect her is by banging a flip-flop on the floor, something that scares me a lot, and to tell the truth it does make me wise up. But she does scold me and yell at me, even if in the middle of the scolding and yelling she realizes that I'm beautiful and she takes me by the head and squeezes me affectionately.

She tells everyone that I'm a kind of *fricken*. The word is a compound of frog and chicken. She says I'm fat like a frog and I have eyes like a chicken's, too far to either side, it looks like I can't see forward, only sideways. She also says that I'm a fish. She shows off to visitors, shouting, "Help! A fish!" and then her friends blow kisses to the fricken and the fish that is me.

She's stopped eating because she misses a person who is my *dad*. The term *dad* is her invention. I'm happy because the less she eats, the more she writes. If she starts to eat she doesn't write. If she starts to read she doesn't write. She has to be completely idle and free and very hysterical for a truly marvelous text to come out of her. That's how she writes the best things. In an ideal state of desperation.

I'm the only thing she has and I do realize that and I like it. She takes off her clothes and bathes and lies down on the bed's edge and I go and lick an arm until she scolds me. It's yummy when the skin is all wet and tastes like soap or lotion. She uses lotions that taste like dried fruits. I like it. I like it. I like it.

She gets up and starts to write naked and suddenly connects her speaker and she gets up from the chair and picks me up and together we dance to "La Bilirrubina" or any song by Juan Luis Guerra or by Rita Indiana or by whoever. It's a playlist for parties that only take place between her and me. The party is here and now.

When this person who is my *dad* was at home she danced only with that person. All three of us naked because I'm always naked. I ran crazy around the living room because that's what I think dancing is. Running and dancing are the same thing to me. When she and my *dad* danced they almost couldn't dance from so much hugging. She misses my *dad* and I miss my *dad*, but the good thing is that she has only me now to act as her source of inspiration so I'll be the one and only protagonist of her books. The whole world will know me.

She cooks up some stews of carrot, radish, and green beans that she shares with me, and since she's obsessive compulsive she cuts twenty-five slices of carrot, twenty-five of radish, and twenty-five of green beans. A stew unique in the world that contains a total of seventy-five vegetable pieces. She gives me a portion of that with my daily rice and my daily sweet potato.

Only once did I get food poisoning and it was with minced turkey, a thing she hasn't spent her money on since then, not even to eat it herself. My eyeballs bulged and I broke out in hives. She shouted, "Help, a fish!" and she started to cry, and called a friend on the phone and snuck a pill quickly into my mouth because I didn't want to swallow it. After a while I felt better and my eyes again looked like what they are, a couple of frog eyes, huge and green and tender.

If she ever has kids that'll be it for me, she'll pour all that mothering into the new baby. She'll make the baby into the protagonist of her books and her poems, she'll take it to readings and to the movies and to the theater, the way she does with me now—she takes me everywhere and people look at her like she's a crazy person with an unhealthy mother complex.

Her girlfriends feel sorry for her because she lives in a rented apartment that costs an arm and a leg. Or something even more valuable—an eye. I also cost an eye, so if you look at it like that the author of this book is a female Oedipus. I'm citing Oedipus because I know that talking about theater consoles and cheers her. Everything to do with theater consoles and cheers her. Because the person who is my *dad* worked in the theater and all that has to do with that medium.

I cost her the equivalent of five months' rent. She'd just come back from a poetry festival in Miami with a little money to subsist on, so it would be a good while before things got bad. But then she got that urge she gets that's like a fit, and she decided the only thing that would make her happy was a newborn Italian greyhound or a newborn French bulldog.

That is the origin of my existence in this story of hers and mine. And no one knows this, not her family, not her friends, not her enemies. I guess that now when the book is published everyone will find out and open their mouths in a sign of astonishment.

I understand that this text, because it's the last, should be conclusive and overwhelming, with an unsettling conflict and denouement, because that's how it happens in almost all the books and in almost all the movies and plays, the final minutes have to be overwhelming. But that's not how this will go, because this is a descriptive text in which I'd like to expound upon my perceptions about human life.

It's odd to watch her interact with her friends. I can tell when it's a true friend who's come over, and I can tell when it's just a friend, or when the person who has come over doesn't interest her in the slightest, or when it's someone she can't stand at all. I can also tell who is family and who's not. Her best girlfriends are her family.

It takes her a long time to read boring books, and sometimes she sneaks around her own conscience and abandons those books halfway through, doesn't even finish them. She reads the books she likes very quickly, in a few hours, but she still never forgets to feed me, give me water, and clean up my urine.

At first she dried my urine with a mopping cloth that she rinsed and wrung out all the time. Then the person who is my *dad* taught her the magic of the newspaper, and since then she hasn't rinsed and wrung out again. She's saved herself work, detergent, and time.

Since the person who is my *dad* left I can feel she's more attached to me. I see her crying and I go over to her skin and I lick her skin softly and she looks at me and thanks me. She says, "My love, my fish, my little fish." That makes her cry more and it makes me howl and lick her more. Again she says, "My love, my fish, my little fish." The scene goes *in crescendo* until she dries her own tears and says, "Enough." Sometimes she's very hard on me and on herself. She's hard when she writes, and she takes revenge for the bad things that happen to her by writing. Not like other writers and artists, who take revenge in other ways.

If she's given something delicious to eat, she gives half to me.

If she copies a new, good movie, she tilts the screen so I can take a look, even though she knows that dogs can't understand movies even if they're as smart as I am.

If she's invited to a party, she takes me.

If she thinks I won't be able to make it because of the sun or the distance she doesn't take me, and she doesn't go either.

We have the party at home.

She celebrates my monthly birthday.

I was born February seventh, so every seventh I turn another month old. And that day I eat the same thing as always, well cooked over a low flame with a lot of water, no salt or oil, and I receive the same love as always, but something tells me it's a special day. Something in her voice and in her eyes.

To write a book whose leitmotif is the bond, affectionate or grotesque, with a pet, in this case a dog, is not a thing she was the first to come up with. Literary history is full of similar examples. Even Anton Chekhov, a man of theater, wrote about a dog, and I'm referring to a very serious story published for children called "Whitebrow." In my case I also have a white brow, like the puppy in Chekhov's story.

Chekhov's tale is about a she-wolf who is able to raise a puppy of another species. The same thing happens in this book, whose author is raising me, I am not of her species, not even close.

Really it's not about that, it's about something quite different, I made that up after she showed me the illustrations.

I know how to get up onto the furniture and I sleep better there than on the floor, even if it's hot. But if she gets up from the bed where she's always reading, or if she turns over in bed, or throws off the covers, or goes to the bathroom to pee, or to the kitchen to knock back a glass of water, or whatever she does, I can't help but open my eyes, prick up my ears, look at her, and follow. I love her. She's my mother.

Counting today, it's been three days since she's gotten up from the bed. I saw her lay down in bed day before yesterday after feeding me and giving me water. She'd taken a bunch of pills from her backpack and swallowed them nervously. She even let me get up onto the bed and shred a pair of pants that are among her favorites. I tore them up not because I'm bad but because I like her smell a lot.

Before she went to sleep I saw she was reading a book by a certain Coetzee, a writer she loves and whose books she drinks like glasses of water. I watched her read from the sofa, on a cushion, and I started falling asleep too. When I woke up she had the book in one hand, on page one hundred and three, and she didn't finish it.

At night she didn't get up, yesterday either. I'm hungry and thirsty. I've gotten up on her bed several times, I've played with her hair and she doesn't wake up. Maybe she needs time. If she needs to sleep several hours for every pill she took, then she'll be asleep at least a year.

Everything that Gilles Deleuze posits in his famous *Alphabet Book*, which begins tidily with the letter A, becomes earth and dust before me. Gilles Deleuze can't stand animals. He's a great philosopher but he can't stand the friendly and familiar treatment of dogs and cats, and as such, for me and for her, he is reduced to dust. I love her. She's my mother. And she is the best writer in the world.

In the division
of property
the French bulldog
got the telephone,
and I kept quiet.

Legna Rodríguez Iglesias (Camagüey, 1984) is a prize-winning Cuban poet, fiction writer, and playwright. She has published widely, including the poetry books *Mi pareja calva y yo vamos a tener un hijo* (Ediciones Liliputienses, 2019), *Miami Century Fox* (Akashic Books, 2017), and Transtucé (Editorial Casa Vacía, 2017); the short story collections *La mujer que compró el mundo* (Editorial Los Libros de La Mujer Rota, 2017) and *No sabe/no contesta* (Ediciones La Palma, 2015); and the novels *Mi novia preferida fue un bulldog francés*, (Editorial Alfaguara, 2017), *Mayonesa bien brillante* (Hypermedia Ediciones, 2015), and *Las analfabetas* (Editorial Bokeh, 2015). Among her literary awards are the Centrifugados Prize for Younger Poets (Spain 2019), the Paz Prize (the National Poetry Series, 2017), the Casa de las Américas Prize in Theater (Cuba, 2016), and the Julio Cortázar Ibero-American Short Story Prize (2011). *Spinning Mill*, a chapbook of her work, has recently appeared in English translation with CardBoard House Press (2019, trans. Katerina Gonzalez Seligmann). She currently lives in Miami where she writes a column for the online journal El Estornudo.